9INE
OF
FOOLS

 Queendom Dreams Publishing

Acknowledgements

As always, I give all honor and thanks unto Jehovah God. For without His grace, no talent that I have been blessed with would come to fruition. I thank Him for the past, present, and the blessings to come.

Thank you to all along my path who have supported me in this journey. For those looking for a list of names this time, no can do. I'd have a whole other book filled with acknowledgements, and I know that's not the book you'd want to read from me. Anyone that's anyone knows who they are and don't need acknowledgment in a book to know how priceless they are in my life because I continually let you know personally.

My readers and fans of The Queen, words will never express the level of gratitude I have for you. Without you, I am just another person writing books. Prayerfully, you will stick with me along my journey and inspire me to want to give you more.

Gotta shout out my Queensbridge family...Family for life.

The Queen

9INE
OF
FOOLS

The Queen

Queendom Dreams Publishing
www.queendomdreamspublishing.com

1

"Mmm, it smells delicious." Ron took a deep breath as he entered the massive white kitchen while knotting his tie. "I love when my beautiful wife fixes me breakfast. Seems like forever."

His wife, Ava, and their youngest son, Rashaun, were sitting at the breakfast table. He leaned over and kissed Ava on the cheek before walking over to check the microwave, stove, double wall oven, convection oven, and lastly, the refrigerator for his serving of the food he saw them eating. While Ron searched the appliances for his breakfast, Ava sat quietly watching him.

"Where's my plate?"

Rashaun smirked.

After swallowing the forkful of food she'd been chewing, Ava put on her most sincere voice and replied, "Oh, I'm sorry, dear. I didn't fix you any. I know you hate reheated food, and I didn't think you'd be up this early." She held up her plate to show what little remained of the breakfast. "But, you're welcomed to finish my plate. I'm already stuffed from the blackened shrimp and grits, omelet with spinach and crabmeat, waffle, and bacon. Whew! I don't think I can eat another bite." She then patted her stomach to stress her point.

"Ten o'clock in the fuckin' morning and you didn't think I'd be up this early? REALLY? REALLY? We're doing this bullshit again, Ava? I bust my ass to provide a good life for this family and your children, but I can't even get a fuckin' plate of food from my wife? This is some bullshit, Ava, and you know it."

Sensing Rashaun was about to go off on his father, Ava placed her hand over his to calm him. She exchanged a reassuring look with their son.

"No, really, Ron, it wasn't intentional. Rashaun had some business he needed to discuss with me before he goes to work on his event happening this evening. Since we were in the kitchen talking, I just started pulling out some pots and pans. I didn't even intend to cook all of this. You know I prefer my oatmeal in the mornings. I can have Guida whip you up something when she gets in, though."

Ron gripped the sides of the marble counter, closed his eyes, and silently counted to ten before yelling, "I don't want the fucking maid to cook for me! I want my wife to cook for me! Is that too damn much to ask? I swear, it seems like you only cook once a fucking year these days. Thirty years of marriage, and you went on strike after this one here was born twenty-five years ago." Ron waved his hand in Rashaun's direction.

"Wow! You must be away from home quite a bit, because even when I'm on the road with my business, I get a good home-cooked meal from Mom at least three times a week, and I don't even live here," Rashaun bragged to agitate his father. "That lobster stuffed ravioli she fixed the other day… Mannnn, that was the best."

"Oh, shut the fuck up! Who asked you anything? Hmph! I'm sure she prepares meals for whoever your father is, as well. Speaking of which, have you ever found him yet?" Ron antagonized at a safe distance from his taller, more muscular son.

Rashaun jumped up from his chair to defend his mother's honor again, but she grabbed his arm.

"Rashaun, there's no need to do anything foolish. Just sit back, because one day soon, you'll own your father's empire." Ava winked at her son and gave him a comforting smile.

"And how exactly will he get my empire? I don't even have

him in my will. Eve is the only one who treats me with respect. If anything, she'll own my empire. She can have anything I own. That's my firstborn and my heart."

"Uh, did you forget that Shara is your firstborn?" Ava asked, chuckling at Ron's foolishness that she had become accustomed to over the years.

"How do I know Shara is actually my daughter? Her mother died before I could get a blood test, and Shara is a fast-ass just like her mother was."

Rashaun leaned over to kiss his mother's cheek. "Sorry, Mom, but I gotta get out of here before I end up knocking that old dude out. Then he wonders why no one can stand his crusty ass. Thankfully, I don't have his name to carry on."

Ron arrogantly laughed. "Did you forget your dumbass has my last name, although your momma obviously gave you your father's first name?"

"Ronald Elliott Johnson, would you shut the fuck up with the stupid shit this morning!" Ava scolded. "Don't nobody want to hear the ramblings of an old man. I know I don't."

"Old man? I don't hear you calling me an old man in the bedroom." Ron laughed, amusing himself as he gyrated his hips to make it clear what he was talking about.

"Ugh! Let me go before I throw up my delicious breakfast that the senile, old nut missed out on. I left a few scraps on my plate. Feel free to be the pig you are. Help yourself to them after I leave." Rashaun turned to Ava. "See you at my seminar later this evening?"

"Wouldn't miss it, my love," Ava replied with a smile.

When Rashaun was gone, Ava stood to clear the table. Ron quickly stopped her to pick the untouched blackened jumbo shrimps left on Rashaun's plate, as well as a few forkfuls of the spinach and crabmeat omelet before breaking off a piece of the waffle Ava had prepared.

Ava laughed. "You're really going to stand there and eat table scraps. You are truly ridiculous, and you better stop speaking to your son like that before one day I let him beat the hell out of you."

"He's a momma's boy. I told you not to breastfeed him for so long. I bet you want him to do something to me so that you can inherit everything."

"Ron, if I wanted to knock you off, I'd simply prepare your meals each day and add something to them. As for *your* empire that you *think* you own, that damn company wouldn't be shit today if it wasn't for me and my creative genius. You didn't even know how to think outside of the box. When I met your ass, you only had a one-bedroom apartment. Although I can't stand this house, we only got this eleven-bedroom mansion as a result of my hard work and ingenuity."

"My company would have been just as successful if I didn't meet you. You were the mailroom clerk, for crying out loud," he reminded her as he often would.

"Whatever! I might have been the mailroom clerk, but you obviously couldn't live without me."

Ron softened up. "That's because you used to always cook for me. I think you put voodoo on me back then," he chuckled, trying to take Ava into his arms.

"You're a damn nut, you know that?" Ava squirmed as she tried to escape his kisses to her neck. "Don't you have someplace to be? And watch your greasy hands before you get them on my clothes."

"Baby, I'm horny. Can we go upstairs for a little while before I head to the office?" Ron asked while sensually rubbing up against Ava's behind.

"Damn, I'm horny, too, but I'm going to reserve my loving for Rashaun's father."

"I'm Rashaun's father," Ron said, still pleading and kissing on Ava.

"Oh, now you're his father but wasn't just ten minutes ago." Ava laughed. She had also become accustomed to Ron's insane pattern of switching up.

"The boy looks just like his handsome dad. Even a blind man can see that. He just pisses me off all the time because he's so disrespectful. All of them are. Especially Shara."

"Ron, you constantly remind Jeremy that he's only your stepson instead of YOUR son, despite your being in his life since he was a year old. You didn't even go to claim Shara from her poor grandparents until three years after her mother died. She was already seven years old, and that only happened because I went to get her once we were married. You have continuously told Rashaun, for all of his twenty-five years of life, that you're not his father just because I didn't name him Ronald Junior. Even though Ariana works to keep our company going, you try to make her live in the shadows of Eve, and Eve doesn't even want any parts of the company."

"But Eve was our first child together. Do you have any idea how spectacular that day was to me when she was born? Every time I think back to that day of you giving me that precious gift, I think about how much in love we were." Ron smiled as he reminisced.

"Well, when I gave birth to Ariana and Rashaun that should have been just as spectacular. Especially when I gave you a son."

"A son that you gave another man's name," Ron said, getting angry again and stepping away from his wife. "How could you do that to me? We had already planned to name our son Ron Junior. Do you know how embarrassed I was telling everyone that our son's name was Ron Junior, only to see the birth certificate with some damn Rashaun? You didn't even have the decency to tell me what you did. You let me go around calling him 'Lil Ron' for all of that time."

"I guess you keep forgetting about that home-wrecking ho that called me in the hospital right after you got the call that I was in labor and left her."

"Why are you bringing up old shit? I told you, I didn't have anything going on with her. I don't know why she did what she did, but you see I fired her immediately after I found out what she did."

Ava rolled her eyes. "Ron, you seem to forget you already confessed to that affair."

"I did no such thing. If I did, it was because you named my son after another man."

"Your stupid ass had your sister, Tracy, pay the girl not to go public with your affair, remember? Tracy is like my friggin' twin. You know she told me because we are that close."

"Just because I paid the girl not to go public with some silly scandal doesn't mean there was any truth to that garbage. I was only trying to protect my family like any real man would."

Ava laughed hysterically. "Oh my God, Ron! You are so full of shit! You fuckin' cried and begged me to forgive you. You told me that she didn't mean shit to you and you only had a momentary lapse in judgment because of my high-risk pregnancy, which disrupted our sex life those last few weeks. Remember that confession?"

Ron shook his head while heading out of the kitchen. "No. No, I don't recall any such confession. Anyhow, I need to get to the office since I can't get a meal or any sex from my wife."

"Have a great day!" Ava called out in a teasing manner.

Ron grumbled, "Yeah, whatever."

2

Leaving from the men's room, Ron returned to his office. It was late, and he was about to wrap things up so he could head home. Before being seen, he overheard the conversation of the two cleaning women.

"Sherita, I don't know when you gonna let that mess go from ya mind. Ain't no Prince Charming gonna come along and take care of you. Me and my husband been together for eleven years now, and we do the teamwork thing. He watches our four kids while I work here at night. I watch the kids during the day while he works at the plant."

"I just don't want to struggle. I want a nice, older man to take care of me."

"Eeew! Why an older man? They're always married."

"I don't care if he's married. As long as he can fuck me good and got money to make it where I don't have to be cleaning up people's houses and offices, I'm good."

"What's the oldest man you ever fucked? Their dicks can't even stay hard."

"How would you know? You ain't ever been with an older man."

"Have you?"

"Sure have," Sherita answered with a proud smile. "I did it with this older white man who I used to clean up for. We'd sneak and get busy with his wife in the house, and she wouldn't have a clue. They had a big house, so it was easy to slip off. Then there was this older black man who owned the grocery store near me. I was like way younger back then, but he'd give me whatever I wanted."

"That's disgusting! You were sexing a child molester?"

"He wasn't a child molester," Sherita defended.

"You said you were way younger. You're only twenty-four now. How old were you and how old was he?"

"What does it matter? It's not like he made me do something I didn't want to do. I wanted to be with him, and he knew how to make me feel good."

"Whatever! My husband is the only man I've ever been with and the only man for me."

"You've been with the same guy since you were fourteen years old. You don't ever feel like you could be missing out on something?"

"Sherita, my husband is everything I need."

"You're pregnant with your fifth child and still have to work to help your husband provide. Say what you want about me, but at least I don't have any children that I have to struggle to take care of."

"Keep fucking all them old men, and you gonna have you a baby soon."

"I don't care, 'cause that means he'll be taking care of me and this nice plump booty." Sherita laughed as she patted her behind.

The conversation was beginning to arouse Ron, and he decided to make his presence known.

"Ladies," he said, briskly walking past them to his office.

"Good evening," they sang in unison, shocked and embarrassed.

"I'm sorry. We thought you were gone for the evening. We can come back and finish later if you'd like," Sherita said, seeming somewhat frightened.

"No need to leave. I'm about to head on out."

One of the ladies disappeared, leaving Sherita to finish cleaning the large open office space in silence. Ron found himself suddenly drawn to her as he watched her bending over while cleaning. He'd seen the cleaning staff a million times before, but he could never recognize any for lack of paying them any attention. Sherita wasn't as beautiful as his wife, but her body was a turn on, and especially now that she pointed out the plumpness of her ass.

Sherita pretended not to see the owner of the company watching her every move. His watching made her want to be with him. She figured Ron to be in his early sixties, but so was the store owner who she'd been involved with when she was just fourteen years old.

"I finished cleaning out there. Is it alright to come in here and start, or should I wait until you go?" she asked.

"You can come in. I'm leaving." After Sherita started busying herself with cleaning his office, he said, "I don't recall seeing you around. Have you been here long?"

Sherita stopped what she was doing to be attentive to Ron's conversation. "Yes, sir. I've been here almost three years now."

"Really?!" Ron asked, surprised. "Well, I appreciate your dedication."

"I'm just thankful to be here. I tried working over at the factory with my momma, but I can't sit in one spot all day."

"Understood. I feel the same way, which is why I travel so much. Do you know my youngest daughter, Ariana? She works here from time to time when she's not trying to pursue an acting career."

"I don't know her personally, but I've seen her a few times. We were told we're not allowed to talk with the executive staff."

Ron seemed surprised by the rule he implemented many years ago.

"Oh well, if anyone says anything about you talking to me, just let them know you have my permission," Ron said, trying to size up the seemingly plump breasts that matched the plump booty that aroused him.

She smiled and replied, "I appreciate it."

"Wasn't there another young lady with you? Where is she?" Ron asked.

He realized they were flirting, and he didn't want to get busted.

"She works on the floor downstairs. We have assigned floors to work. She was just up here running her mouth for a minute. I figured I'd help her out when I get done up here."

"Okay, well, I won't hold you up any longer… What's your name?" he asked, immediately contradicting himself.

"Sherita. My name is Sherita Walker."

"Sherita Walker," Ron repeated in a flirtatious manner. "Nice to meet you, Miss Sherita."

"Thank you. You, as well," she said, smiling.

The shyness in her eyes upon meeting his eyes enhanced his attraction to her. He didn't want to end the conversation not knowing if he'd see her again. After ending his last affair two months prior, he swore to himself it would be the last time he'd cheat on his wife. However, with so much disrespect swirling around in his household, it felt more like a battlefield than a home.

"Miss Sherita, if I were to kiss you, would you be offended?"

Sherita was shocked by Ron's boldness. Despite her shock, her nipples hardened from the anticipation of his kiss. Rather than answer with words, she stepped closer to where he sat on the edge of his desk. He stood up to take her into his arms and kissed her as if he had been longing for her kiss for quite a while. His hands took measurements of her body, and he liked what he felt. While kissing her, he slipped a hand underneath her uniform top and then underneath her bra to squish her healthy-sized, natural breast. His hand left there to bypass the elastic band on her pants so he could cup one of her ass cheeks. She groaned a little, but he wasn't sure if he was making her uncomfortable or not. Nonetheless, he didn't care. He had one more measurement to make, and that was her vaginal cavity.

He had to know if she was tight or loose.

As much as he loved his wife and making love to her, she was far from having a tight vagina, and she had zero interest in getting a procedure done to tighten it back up for him. His obsession with fucking tight pussy had led him to have countless affairs during the last twenty-eight years of their thirty-year marriage. Somehow, after watching his wife give birth to their first daughter together, Eve, he could never seem to experience that same tight feeling he did with his wife.

Though his cheating on his wife almost their entire marriage was despicable, the worst thing he felt he'd done was to get involved with one of Shara's acquaintances. Shara had just started college, and Ron had taken the long drive to her school to drop her off some items she insisted he bring her. In her rude, disrespectful, typical self, she volunteered Ron to give another young lady a ride to her home because the nineteen-year-old had been expelled for public intoxication. One thing led to another, and they ended up stopping at a hotel before he could complete the two-and-a-half-hour drive. That relationship lasted over a year, which was the time when the girl found out Ron was seeing yet another young lady. That's when Shara was told about both affairs and became his public enemy to the tenth power. Although Shara never shared the details with her stepmother Ava, whom she adored and didn't want to hurt, she'd always been on a crusade for Ava to take all of Ron's money and leave him lonely and pathetic.

As he reminisced, his fingers explored deeper into Sherita's tight, hot, wet orifice. He was ready to strip her down naked, but they were both startled when they heard Sherita's name being called out by her co-worker. They quickly pulled away from one another and gave the illusion of being busy. The co-worker saw Ron was still present, sitting behind his desk and looking annoyed.

"Do you work on this floor?" Ron angrily asked.

Knowing she was neglecting her duties, she became

terrified of losing her job. "No, sir. I work downstairs. I was just checking up on Sherita because sometimes we work on a floor together to get it done quicker."

"Seems when I interrupted you earlier, you were doing a whole lot of talking and very little of the job you're paid to do."

Sherita turned to look at Ron and then to her six-month-pregnant friend, afraid she was about to be fired.

"I'm sorry, sir. I promise it won't happen again."

"If this is not your floor, don't let me see you back on it again."

"No, sir, you won't see me on this floor again," she said, quickly heading back towards the stairwell.

Sherita didn't know what to do or say. Ron was clearly angry.

"Uh, should I come back over there, or should I just finish cleaning and go?"

Despite being tense and angered by the co-worker's intrusion, Ron unbuckled his pants and opened them, then motioned for Sherita to come to him. When she was close enough, he lifted her top and bra to allow his mouth access to her nipple. He guided her hand to his open trousers, where Sherita instinctively stuck her hand inside of his underwear to take hold of his slightly hardened tool. She was impressed with its size, and that made him smile.

He leaned back in his oversized executive chair and gave her the green light to do whatever she wanted. Wanting to please him, she decided she'd give him head after she had his cock out of his pants. She assumed the position, dropping to her knees. As her head bobbed up and down, she tried to take him as deep into her throat as she could. He was especially impressed with the fact that the wavy ponytail she was sporting was her real hair, which allowed him to freely dig into the roots of her hair to help control the pace of her bobbing. It didn't take him long to explode inside her mouth. Uncomfortable with swallowing, she looked for somewhere to dispose of the mouthful of hot semen. However, after noticing Ron's disapproving look, she forced herself to swallow. Only then did his expression soften and his body relax.

Ron found some napkins in his desk to clean himself up and then packed to leave.

"What time do you begin working?" he asked.

"I usually work seven to midnight."

"You're only part-time?"

"Yes, sir."

"How do you survive?"

Her forced smile made it evident that she was embarrassed to answer. "I live at home with my momma and my two younger sisters. We all contribute what we can to pay the bills. Oh, and two of my girl cousins live with us since their momma died about eight years ago."

"What part of town do you live in?"

"We live in the Bottoms, in Griffin. Our home ain't much, but don't nobody bother us over there."

"Aren't those the government houses they built a few years back?"

"Yes, sir. Walls are paper thin, and you can hear your neighbor sneeze. A train passes by like every hour, but it beats where we used to live."

"How old are your sisters and mother?" he interrogated.

"I have a sister, Shirleen. She's twenty. She doesn't work, but she goes to the Community College. She wants to work here when she finishes school. My sister Sherrell is eighteen, and she works at the diner near our home. My cousin Tonjenae is twenty-one. She works with my momma, Shirley, at the factory. Then there's Tonjenae's sister, Toni, who's nineteen and a clerk at the local grocery store."

"How old is your mother? Where's your father?"

Sherita frowned. "My momma is thirty-nine. She had me when she was just fifteen. Our father was in the streets, and one day he got shot. He didn't die, but my momma wanted us away from there. So, she moved us from Tuscaloosa, Alabama, to Griffin, Georgia."

"Isn't that a long commute for you?"

"It is, but I like my job. Plus, the pay here is much better than where we live."

"Why not just move here into Atlanta?"

"It's way too expensive. Besides, Momma gets nervous in big cities. Too many folks."

"So do you have a boyfriend?" Ron quizzed.

"No. Can't seem to find one of those these days."

"Well, who takes care of your needs for you?"

Sherita looked down at her rundown shoes. "I have to take care of myself when I take a bath."

Ron grinned. "Oh really?"

"Yes, sir."

"Would you like for me to help you with that right now?"

She bashfully smiled. "I think I would like that."

He beckoned for her to stand between his chair and the desk. She did as he instructed. Once she was within reach, he inserted his fingers back into her tight cavity, while lifting her top and bra to give her nipples some attention. No doubt about it he was making her feel good. With his office door and blinds still open, she became a bit nervous when he slid one of her pants legs off. She was worried her co-worker would come to check on her again since she had already been missing for at least an hour.

Ron laid Sherita back slightly on the desk so he could orally stimulate her. She squeezed her breasts as his tongue flicked her clit. His fingers continued their exploration deep inside her cave, and when her body released a mound of cum onto his fingers, he decided to suck it all up.

"I bet you can't do that to yourself, now can you?"

Still trying to catch her breath, she answered, "No, sir."

Ron debated on inserting his erection inside of the young, tight orifice, but he was still hoping to engage in a night of passion with his wife once he got home. He decided on a few thrusts to try her on and then he'd quit, a skill he had mastered over the years. He loved how he had to push his way inside her. In full control of himself, he managed to pull out of her as planned. However, she was pleading for more because she wanted him so bad.

"I'm sorry, I have to get home to my wife. Tomorrow. Come see me tomorrow. I'll get a hotel room for us."

Sherita was sorely disappointed but had no room to argue. So, she gave her number to him and agreed to meet him the next day.

3

"You need to take that wildebeest out camping one day and put him out of his misery once and for all."

"Nah, drive him way up in the mountains in North Carolina or Tennessee and leave him there. Whatever will happen will happen."

"Jeremy owns a defense contracting company. He can be target practice for his clients."

"You guys are so cruel." Ron heard Ava laugh. "Be quiet with all that crazy talk before your father comes in and hears you all plotting death."

Ron felt his breath escaping him. He couldn't believe he walked in on his wife and children plotting his death. Despite his brief escapade in the office, he stopped to get flowers and his wife's favorite candy, Godiva Chocolates, to shower her with love. Instead, he got the opportunity to hear how his wife and children greatly despised him…to the point of killing him off.

As he stood out of view in the corner, he debated on whether or not to let them know he heard of their plot to murder him, causing them to all benefit from the wealth he had built. The thought infuriated him. At that moment, he felt determined to find a way to get his wife out of his life and leave her penniless. Even if he had to die, he'd make sure she got nothing.

While standing frozen in his thoughts, he hadn't realized Shara's voice was getting nearer to him right before she turned the corner.

"Would you look at this jackass over here eavesdropping."

"Shara! Stop being so disrespectful to your father," Ava scolded.

Ron finally found his voice. "Every last one of you is disrespectful to me. Here I come home to shower my wife with love, and instead, I hear you…hear you…"

Overcome with grief, Ron couldn't finish his sentence.

"Oh, so the Tin Man does have a heart, huh?" Rashaun chuckled, then turned to kiss his mother goodbye. "I'll call you in the morning. I could use your infinite wisdom on this new project I'm considering."

"That's fine," Ava quickly said to Rashaun, wanting to turn her attention back to her grieved husband. "Ron, why are you so upset? If you were listening, then you heard me say that you and I are long overdue for a little getaway. I think a few days at a cabin in the mountains would be great for us."

"Great for us? Who, you and the kids? Do you think you're going to kill me off, take all my money, and go live happily ever after? You better think again!"

Everyone looked confused.

"Kill you? What are you talking about, Ron?"

"I heard you and the kids talking about it. You want to take me up to the mountains to put me out of my misery. But, I got something for every one of your asses. I am going to have the last laugh somehow, someway, and none of you will get a dime."

Ava and the kids stood there with a confused look on their faces as Ron threw down the flowers and chocolates and left the house.

"Momma, I think Daddy heard us talking about putting Fluffy down," Eve said, referring to their sixteen-year-old dog.

"No! You think?"

"Now that you mention it, I remember Daddy saying something about putting him out of his misery, and that's the same wording I used…putting the wildebeest out of his misery." Shara laughed. "How could he not realize we were talking about the dog? If he heard me say that, then he should have heard you, Mom, when you said that dog means the world to him since Fluffy is the only one that doesn't talk back to him."

"Oh Lord, I told y'all Daddy was losing his mind," Eve said. "I'm going to see if I can reach him on his cell. He usually answers my calls."

Ava didn't know whether to laugh or cry. On the one hand, she thought it was funny that her husband was paranoid to the point where he thought someone was conspiring to kill him to gain the wealth that she pretty much already controlled. On the other hand, she wanted to cry because she missed out on a romantic night and possibly him thinking he had yet another valid excuse to crawl between some woman's legs. Ava was sick of dealing with the infidelity and women threatening her life because they wanted to be the new Mrs. Johnson. It was even more annoying because their children always seemed to find out before Ava. As a result, none of them treated their father with respect, and Ava always had to play referee.

"Daddy's not answering," Eve announced. "You gonna be alright, Mom? I have to get going home. I have a business to run."

"Go on. I'll be fine. You all can get going. I'm sure your father will be home soon."

"Really, Mom? You're gonna act like you don't know he's using this bullshit as an excuse to be a ho!" Shara laughed.

"Takes a ho to know a ho, and you definitely know your hos," Ariana commented, laughing.

"Shut up!" Shara also laughed. "I'm not a ho. I just like sex. Unadulterated, freaky sex."

"That's all gravy, but your little brother's friends and your aunt's men are off limits," Ariana rebutted.

"I have never slept with Rashaun's friends."

"And the lie detector has determined…THAT IS A LIE! Did you forget about that time you let two of his friends feel you up one night?" Eve reminded her.

"But I didn't sleep with them. Touching and sex are not the same."

"What about Aunt Tracy's men? You've been stealing her men…since…since… Eeew! That's disgusting. I get sick of you embarrassing me with your shenanigans," Ariana told Shara.

"I get it honestly from your father," Shara laughed. "Let's just say, whoredom runs in the genes."

"Must be from that lady who birthed you, because you're in a league all by yourself."

"Eve! Hush that talk!" Ava scolded. "That's very disrespectful."

"Relax, Mom. I'm not offended. It is what it is. Some ho lady screwed your ho husband, and a ho daughter was produced. Ta-da!" Shara laughed, pointing to herself.

"Well, it's disrespectful to me. I raised you for thirty of your thirty-seven years. And stop referring to yourself as a whore. You are not a whore."

"Sorry, Mom," Shara said, remorseful as she hugged her.

"Yes, she is!" Ariana yelled out simultaneously, laughing.

Ava just shook her head. "You all staying here tonight? I'm going upstairs to relax my nerves and watch some television for a change."

"Nah, I'm heading out. I can't stand this house," Ariana said, turning up her nose.

"Exactly how I feel. I don't understand why you two needed to get an eleven-bedroom home AFTER all of your kids are grown. That makes no sense," Eve cosigned.

"This was your father's bright idea. He thought we'd need a place big enough for grandchildren. Only one granddaughter from Jeremy. Who would have thought it? I just knew I'd have at least ten grandbabies by now." Ava chuckled. "I thought for sure Shara would have given me at least three."

Shara laughed the loudest. "Now that's funny. I'm still

thinking about moving back to Jersey. Jeremy's up there still. Ariana's planning to move to New York to buckle down on her acting career. Georgia's not for me and definitely not babies."

"Shara, you live in a different country for six months at a time. How are you moving back to Jersey?" Eve asked.

"I want that to be my home base instead of Georgia," she answered. "I grew up in Jersey, not Georgia."

"You know damn well Aunt Tracy don't want you moving back to Jersey near her, taking her men from her," Ariana reminded.

"If they were willing to lay down with me, then that means they were never her men," Shara shot back.

"Umm, David was her husband, and Paul was going to be her second husband. How do you figure?" Ava asked.

"Please! David only married her so no one would know he was pimping young girls. And Paul? Well, I was trying to do her a favor to see if he was on the up and up…if he was trustworthy before she made the mistake of marrying him, too."

Eve looked at Shara as if she were crazy. "I bet that's the bullshit you tell yourself to help you sleep at night. Pimp or not, that is your cousin's father. That's why David Junior doesn't want to come around our family."

"What are you talking about?! He just doesn't want to come around your stuck-up ass. Lil David and I hang out all the time. He even came to hang out with me in Punta Cana."

"That's still disgusting," Ariana snarled.

"Please, me and Big David… that was like almost twenty years ago. Lil David ain't tripping about it. I don't know why y'all are," Shara defended. "Anyhow, I'm out. I got things to do in the morning, and y'all need to get busy tracking your daddy, with the community dick, down so you can make him feel stupid when you tell him no one was plotting to kill him."

"How could you talk so crass about our father like that? Community dick? Now that's uncalled for, and it's a slap in the face to Momma," Eve said.

"Don't worry about my feelings being bruised by true words. Be more concerned with my feelings on how the words became true." Ava stoically shook her head.

"Mom, I think since we're all grown now, we need to get together and discuss your exit strategy. This is insane. You're too youthful looking and too hip to be saddled down with a man like Daddy. We'll always love him, but you deserve so much better. You'll have most of everything he owns anyhow. We all are doing well, so you don't have to put up with his silly shit anymore," Ariana said, hugging her beloved mother.

"See, Ari gets it. She and I, we see eye to eye. Eve got her head stuck so far up Daddy's ass that she still can't see him for who he is," Shara said, getting hyped.

"My head is not stuck up Daddy's ass. For your information, I do agree, and I know Jeremy and Rashaun feel the same. I just hate when you rub Daddy's dirt in Momma's face by constantly reminding her of his dirt."

"No, dear, your dad does a good job of that on his own. No one should have to lie or tiptoe around the truth. No one. And those days of lying to myself, I stopped doing that long ago. I honestly haven't decided what I want to do about my marriage yet. It's not easy to throw away over thirty years together. I noticed he's been trying to hold it together lately, so it's hard to say right now. That's why I thought us going away might have been good, but that situation just went way left." Ava chuckled. "Now, if he goes out and does something else stupid to justify his perception of our conversation… I don't know. And, on that note, goodnight. I love you, and get home safely."

Ava started heading towards the stairs.

"So, we don't get any hugs and kisses goodbye?" Shara playfully pouted with her arms extended for their mother.

With a warm smile, Ava returned to receive the much-needed embrace from her three daughters.

4

"Girl, I can't believe you just got busy with the owner. I like to died when I saw that shit," Sherita's co-worker, Lola, whispered loudly, extra giddy. "We was just talking about that."

"Shhh! Be quiet," Sherita whispered although they were seated inside of her car.

"Was it good?"

"I think so."

"What do you mean, you think so?"

"I mean, he started something and then said he needed to get home to his wife. The whole thing was awkward. I didn't know how to feel. I didn't know if I refused, would I be fired or not. It wasn't bad, but I feel like I didn't have a choice."

"Would you want to do it again with him?"

Sherita thought and smiled. "Hell yeah! He got a nice-sized dick. When he put that shit in me, I was ready to explode right then. He got skills."

Lola giggled like a schoolgirl. "You not worried about his wife none?"

"Oh my Lord, I wouldn't want her to find out. Not even his daughter. I'd lose my job."

"Well, maybe he'll see you in the office at night after everyone's gone. Who's gonna know it? You ain't had a real dick in a minute. You better get yours. Do you, boo!"

"You're right. He did say something about getting a hotel room tomorrow. I don't know when. He just told me that he'd call me."

"Girl, maybe he'll throw a few extra dollars in your

direction."

"That would be wonderful. Trying to survive on two-hundred-and-fifty dollars a week minus taxes and needing a shitload of gas to get here each day is rough. I damn near have to give my momma everything I make, and I'm trying to save up to get a new pair of work shoes. Hell, I'd be happy if he bought me a pair."

"You don't get to go out and party down in Griffin?"

"Girl, please! The only time we party in Griffin is if someone's having a birthday the same time they get their taxes or have extra money left over from something. Maybe every few months we put some money together and ride up this way, but we can't buy no damn drinks because they're too high. Men won't buy you a cup of water but always want somebody's number."

"Why don't you move to Atlanta? Maybe you can find a full-time job and a man."

"They say the ratio of women to men is like nine to one, which means we'll all be sharing one man who won't do shit for us. Living inside of Atlanta is just too damn expensive. I would love to have a place here and not drive over an hour each way to only earn fifty dollars per day. If I'm gonna be sharing some man, though, he better be taking care of me."

"Hopefully, Mister Bossman will help you get a full-time position here since you've been here for a while. With regards to that nine-to-one crap, that's bullshit. Trust me, I'm the only one with my husband. He ain't even thinking about being with no one else."

Sherita bit the sides of her tongue to keep from reminding Lola of that baby scare a year ago involving an alleged mistress. The paternity test came back negative, but it was still proof that her husband cheated on her. She also didn't want to remind Lola of the few times when her husband went missing for a night or two…even a week, then returned saying she needed to learn a lesson and appreciate what she has.

Stories like these that Sherita would often hear made her prefer dealing with older men because they were direct, to the point, and didn't play games. She always knew her place with them. Not only that, but they'd give money or gifts without her having to see them that often. She tried dealing with a guy her age once, and that was a disaster. He always wanted her to buy him stuff or pay his cell phone bill. Eventually, she learned that he was going around calling himself a pimp and bragging about all his hos taking care of him. She was devastated. From then on, she stuck with older men.

"I'm glad you're happy," Sherita warmly responded to Lola's delusional babbling.

Lola reached over as much as she could with her extended belly and the console between them and hugged Sherita.

It was almost one in the morning, and Sherita realized that once again, Lola's husband failed to pick her up from work, which meant Sherita would have to go out of her way to give Lola a ride to Austell since no public transportation was running. Sherita was hungry and exhausted, but she didn't want to stop to get any food because she knew she would have to offer some to Lola, who never refused food.

Sherita dropped Lola off at 1:30 a.m. without receiving any offer of gas money for the thirty-minute ride, and no surprise to Sherita, Lola's husband's car was not in the parking lot of their apartment community. During the thirty-minute ride, her husband hadn't made one attempt to call Lola nor had he answered any of Lola's calls to him. Sherita wanted to rub it in Lola's face since she liked to believe she didn't share her husband with other women, but she knew that would be mean-spirited to do.

She wanted to stop off at the first Waffle House she could find but knew she'd be super tired driving that one-and-a-half-hour ride home alone, especially on a full stomach. So, she opted for the 24-hour McDonald's drive-thru. While she waited in the long line for her order, her phone rang with an unfamiliar number. It made her anxious about who'd be calling her that time of night and why. She had everyone she knew already programmed into her phone.

"Hello," she cautiously answered after turning down the volume on her radio that was helping to keep her awake.

"Were you sleeping?"

"No. Who's this?"

"This is Ron. Ron Johnson. Is this Sherita?"

"Oh!" She lit up, happy to hear from him. "Oh wow! Yes, this is Sherita."

"You sound happy to hear from me. That pleases me."

She couldn't stop smiling. "Yes, I'm just surprised. I didn't expect to hear from you tonight."

"Well, I couldn't stop thinking about you. So, I went on and got us a room near the airport, and I was hoping that maybe if you're not too tired, you could ride back up this way to see me and perhaps finish what we started."

"Well, I haven't had a chance to make it home yet. We sat waiting almost an hour for Lola's ride, and then I had to end up driving her all the way to Austell myself. I just stopped at McDonald's to grab some food since I haven't eaten since lunch."

"Oh no! That's not good. Go ahead and grab your food. I think everything is pretty much closed. I'm at the Marriott Gateway. You can pick up a key at the front desk."

She was doing cartwheels inside, but then it hit her. "Oh, wait, I just realized I don't have any change of clothes. I only have this funky uniform that I've been cleaning in all night. I'll have to go home for a change of clothes first."

"Don't you worry yourself about that. I'll have a nice hot bath waiting for you when you get here, and I'll order you up some new clothes in the morning. Later, I'll take you shopping."

YES!!! Sherita wanted to get out of the car and breakdance from her excitement.

She recomposed herself and calmly answered, "I guess that'll be fine."

"Great! I'll see you when you arrive. Drive safely."

"I will," she responded before ending the call.

She was so thankful for the opportunity to be Ron Johnson's mistress that she didn't know what to do. She'd been the mistress to many, but none were on Ron's level. The older white man she used to clean for would slide her an extra hundred dollars a week behind his wife's back. The older black man with the grocery store simply allowed her to have free items out of his store whenever she wanted. But, back then, she thought like a fourteen-year-old, and in reality, those items never amounted to much. In her almost twenty-four years of living, she had never been a guest at a Marriott. She'd used a lobby bathroom once or twice, but that was it. She had seen her fair share of highway-side motels from the inside, but something of this caliber was a first. And she was even more amazed at the thought of him canceling his romantic night with his wife to be with her.

When she entered the beautiful, spacious suite, she heard soft jazz playing in the background, the type of jazz she figured most older people would prefer. She was amazed at the size of the hotel room and had yet to see a bed. She pushed open the French doors to the bedroom and saw Ron resting peacefully on the king-sized bed. She looked to the other side of the room and spied the massive tub with tea candles lit up all around it, rose petals floating in the water, and a single glass of champagne along with a plate of chocolate-dipped strawberries set to the side. The sight was a beautiful one, and she couldn't believe it was prepared for her by a man she'd just officially met hours before.

She debated on waking him or getting in the hot bath he had prepared for her. Thinking about how hideous she was looking and how funky smelling she must have been, Sherita decided on taking a bath before waking him. After finding the toilet to empty her bladder, she stripped out of her uniform. Little did she know, Ron's eyes opened just in time to see her beautiful silhouette sashay across the room to the tub. He was tempted to let her know he was awake and watching her, but thought against it. He allowed the fiscally disadvantaged woman to have her princess moment. Ron could tell she was having a sensual moment in the water by the gentle splashing along with faint moaning.

Ready for her to get out of the tub to join him on the bed, he quietly raised his upper body up on his elbow and watched her until she noticed him up. She seemed embarrassed when she realized he had been watching her.

"Glad to see you're enjoying yourself. I didn't want to disturb you," Ron said with a smile.

She took that as her cue to end her bath. She stood from the water and collected the towel lying on the side to dry herself and her wet hair. She dropped the damp towel to the floor, grabbed her champagne glass, and seductively walked over to Ron…as she had seen done in movies.

"Wow! You are fucking beautiful!"

"Thank you," she answered before gulping down the last of her champagne.

"The bottle is on the dresser in the bucket."

He watched the beautiful roundness of her ass as she walked away from him to collect the champagne. She placed the bucket on the nightstand, and then Ron sat up to pour her another glass. She took a large sip, set the glass down, then climbed onto the bed and onto Ron. He laid wearing only a robe. She opened his robe and rested her firm breasts against his chest, and their tongues attempted to get reacquainted. He massaged her buttocks while pressing her against his erection.

"Damn, you're beautiful," he whispered again.

He sat up on the bed, leaning her back just enough to allow his mouth the ability to devour her pointed nipples. He slipped his fingers in between their bodies to give him access to tickle her clit. Her breaths became heavy, allowing an escaped moan. Without warning, he flipped her on her back and spread her thighs to bury his face in the depths of her ocean. The performance he was giving in that moment was like the entrée to the appetizer he provided back in his office. She didn't know if it was the champagne going to her head or what, but she certainly wasn't prepared for the beast he had just unleashed on her. She grabbed a pillow, covered her face, and screamed into it as her thigh muscles involuntarily seized from the powerful orgasm.

When he could tell her body was finally relaxing, he gently kissed his way back up her body to her lips, grabbed hold of one of her recovering thighs, and used his other hand to guide his train into her station. He could feel her entire body immediately tighten and then relax once he fully inserted himself inside of her. He looked into her eyes as her reactions changed with each of his strokes. Every now and again, he would kiss her. He wanted to make love to her. The love he was supposed to be making to his wife… the wife who was plotting to kill him.

5

"You wanna talk about last night?" Sherita asked, half annoyed when Ron woke up and cuddled up behind her.

Her question caused him to turn away. He couldn't believe what happened himself. One moment, he was tenderly stroking this young, beautiful, sexy woman, and the next, he was rolling over boo-hoo crying and yelling to his wife, who was not in the room. He wanted to know how she could be plotting to kill the man who gave her everything. He additionally yelled that none of those hos ever meant a thing to him and could never take her place. He wanted to know why she couldn't understand that she's the only woman that he could ever love. He cried himself to sleep, completely forgetting about Sherita.

"I'm sorry about that. I didn't mean for that to happen."

"Who's trying to kill you? Your wife?"

"Yes, but I don't want to talk about it. I guess I should have talked to someone about what's going on before getting you involved."

Sherita agreed in her mind. She couldn't believe how Ron took her to the brink of heaven and then just dropped her to hell the way he did. That was more painfully disappointing than the few strokes he gave her in his office. She couldn't help but wonder if he had 'old man issues' down there that interfered with his performance, making him such a superb pussy eater.

Ron jumped up and threw on his clothes. Then he reached into his pants pocket, pulled out five one-hundred-dollar bills, and laid them on the nightstand.

"I'm sorry, I have to go. I have things I need to deal with

at home. I don't mean to make you feel like a hooker or anything, but I did promise to take you shopping this morning. Order breakfast, whatever you want. It'll charge to the room. Again, I'm sorry. I really would like to make it up to you. It'll just have to be after I deal with home. We can't have a repeat of last night."

Sherita smiled. "So, you do want to see me again? I thought I did something wrong that set you off."

Ron sat on the side of the bed near Sherita. "You did absolutely nothing wrong. The timing is just bad. You're a beautiful and sexy woman who I couldn't stop thinking about when I left the office. I thought about all the many ways I wanted to please you, and one day soon, I will. I promise. I will admit, your only fault is indirectly reminding me of how I felt when I first met her over thirty-one years ago. She, too, had worked for my company, and I didn't even know she existed. What's even crazier, the hair type is almost the same. The two of you don't look alike nor have the same build. You just reminded me of her," Ron said, shrugging.

"Wow! I'm not sure how to feel about that, but I do want you to know that I enjoy being with you. Even though I don't know what the finale feels like *yet*, I have enjoyed the entertainment thus far. And that bath, this room, the champagne… I'm happy and want to do whatever I can to make you happy. If that means being patient and waiting, then that's what I'm gonna do."

Ron cupped Sherita's face and passionately kissed her.

"I gotta get going. Be sure to order you some breakfast. Just call the front desk. Oh, by the way, the room is booked for two nights. Feel free to stay tonight, as well. Who knows, I might be back tonight."

"I'd like that."

Ron dug into his pocket and pulled out another hundred.

"Here, take the night off tonight so you can enjoy your stay here today, even if I don't make it back."

"Wow! But who's going to clean the office tonight?"

"I'll get that handled. You just enjoy."

Sherita cringed as she sat up straight in the bed. "Is it okay if I invite my sisters and my cousins to come up and hang with me today? It's kind of no fun with no one to share it with."

"I'll tell you what. Since tomorrow is Saturday and it's the weekend, I'll go ahead and lock this room in until Sunday or maybe even Monday. That way, you can hang out here in Atlanta with your family. Just charge your meals and drinks to the room. It'll go on my account. And if I make it back, I'll get another room, and maybe you can sneak away to see me."

Sherita jumped off of the bed and into Ron's unexpected arms to hug and kiss him. She even cried happy tears as she thanked him over and over again.

As quick as he was out the door, Sherita was calling her sisters and cousins to ride up and join her.

6

Upon stepping out of the elevator in the Marriott, Ron ran into a large crowd. He wondered what was going on but then saw a sign saying there was a psychic readers' convention. He laughed at the thought.

"Sir, would you like a free sample reading?" a cheery-faced young lady asked him.

He laughed cockily. "You're supposed to be the psychic, so you should already know the answer to your question."

She also laughed. "Unfortunately, I wasn't gifted. I'm only an usher. I direct people who would like a reading to our psychics."

Still in good spirits, Ron shared, "I remember my mother always scolding us to stay away from psychics, witches, and voodoo. She was a church lady. She said that stuff was the devil."

"No, sir. There are even scriptures in the Bible that speak about our spiritual gifts. But, like any other person who possesses a gift, they have to eat and keep a roof over their heads, which is why some charge fees."

"I'm a businessman, so I understand that. You know what? What the hell, let's do it. I have some things I would like answers for anyhow." Ron chuckled although he was serious.

"Great! You won't regret it. I'll put you with the one I think is best. She's with someone right now, but she's definitely worth the wait. I tried them all out, and she was the only one who knew I went to each of them asking the same questions."

"Wow! That's impressive." Ron smiled. "I'll trust your experiment."

It seemed like forever waiting for Madame Juniót, but as quickly as Ron took a seat in front of her, she instinctively spat in her second-generation French accent, "Hmmm, the man-whore."

Ron was ready to bolt up from the hot seat that he found himself sitting in.

"Sit! Don't run. You come for the truth, you get the truth."

"Why would you call me a man-whore when you don't even know me? I haven't said a word."

"You are, and I don't have to know you. It's written all over you." Madame Juniót made a circular hand motion towards Ron. "Anyone can see that you are a married man on paper only. You always have many, many women, and that is a man-whore. Now, that is the end of your free sample. If you want a more in-depth reading, we go into my tent for privacy."

Ron was stunned. He wanted to curse the woman and leave, but in less than two minutes, he knew she had to be the real deal.

She stood and walked toward her tent, then turned and said, "I'll be waiting inside. Time is money. The longer you sit out here will eat into your forty-five-minute reading. I already know the thirty-minute reading won't be enough for you."

She went into the tent. Ron sat another two minutes before curiosity overcame him and he, too, entered the tent.

"You now have forty-three minutes left. That costs ninety dollars."

Ron pulled out a hundred-dollar bill and handed it to her before taking the seat she pointed at for him to sit. No change was offered as she put the money away.

"You have a lot of questions about your marriage, but I'm not sure why you have questions when you keep doing stupid stuff to make your whole family hate you."

"So it's true? My family does hate me?"

"Mister, you didn't need a psychic to tell you that. You ugly to your family. You a man-whore and not nice to your wife or family. You are mean in business. Your wife has been your center, but now you throw it all away to create a new great nation that shall rise up. I see the number nine. Not quite sure what that is just yet."

"Are my wife and children trying to kill me? I heard them saying it when they thought I wasn't home."

"Did you hear that? Did you really hear that, or do you believe that's what you heard?"

"I believe I really heard that."

"You're wrong! Your wife was your center."

"You already said that, but what's that supposed to mean?"

"You're a man-whore who found someone to move your wife from your center. Something you just did moved your wife from the center, and now you seek a new great nation. Again, I see the number nine."

"I'm really confused," Ron said, getting frustrated by the name calling.

"Who did you bring into your life yesterday or today?"

Ron thought about the question, and before he could answer, Madame Juniót responded, "Exactly. You have created damage that cannot be undone, and this person caused you to lose your wife, your center, your balance of every area of your life. As such, you will lose everything."

"So, my wife gets mad over this one piece of ass and thinks she's going to strip me of everything? Trust me, that'll never happen. I built this empire long before I ever heard her name. She can't get shit. The kids are grown. She might get a little spousal support, but that won't be much. And if she thinks she'll find a way to kill me to get all my money, she messed with the wrong dude. Yeah, she needs to know she can be easily replaced. It's not like she does shit for me anyhow. I can't even get a meal from my wife. I gotta beg for sex, and then she's pissed about me fucking other younger, sexier, pretty girls? Center? I think she's been the center of my headaches and frustrations. Even when I wanted to move my business from New Jersey to Georgia, I had to let her know that I own this company and it was my decision.

"I wasn't trying to replace my wife with Sherita, but if Ava wants to fight with me and thinks she'll get half of what I built, she's a fool."

"Please! Please! Enough!" she yelled to shut his annoying ramblings up. "Shuffle that deck of cards and turn over the top three cards. There will be your path."

Ron did as he was told. The first card was death.

"Oh, hell no! This is some bullshit," he yelled. "So, that bitch and those kids really think they're going to get away with killing me? That's how they think they're going to get every fuckin' thing?"

"Please! Enough! The death card is not a literal card. It means something will come to an end. Perhaps your marriage, but it no mean that you die. Turn the next card, and it will help tell the story."

Ron turned over the second card, and it was the fool.

"And what's that supposed to mean?"

"Seems to explain itself. You move other women into the center position to assume your wife's role and want to understand the fool card behind the death card?" Madame Juniót hysterically laughed, but Ron was not at all amused. "Something foolish causes the death of something extremely significant in your life. Turn the last card to see the outcome."

"Death is not the outcome?"

"No, I tell you death don't mean you die and people bury you in a grave. You might wish for a physical death based on what your outcome is, but that's not what it is. I'll say it like you know business. The first card is like your… how you say… situation. Your second card is like what you do about it…"

"Action?" Ron asked.

"Yes! Exactly! And your third card is how it will result."

"So, it can still be a good ending? At least the death card wasn't the result card," he said, cheering up and trying to be optimistic.

"That would have been very bad, but let's see."

Ron turned over the final card, which was the hangman.

"Oh well, maybe death would have been better," Madame Juniót said, again amused.

"What does that mean?"

"Hangman has many meanings, as well, depending on what came before it. Looking at the whole picture, you had a bad situation, you did bad to make it worse, and now this is what you are left with."

"How can I make a bad situation better so I that don't make it worse?"

"When you have a scale, you put much on it, and sometimes it doesn't move the center. But then, you put the lightest thing… say a feather, and it breaks the whole scale. That's what you just did. That is why I asked did you really hear or do you believe you hear. And then poof! You added the feather on what you believe you hear. I can only suggest you try talking, but that really means nothing because you have already decided on your wife's replacement."

"I'm not marrying no damn Sherita! She is nowhere on my wife's level. Not even back when I first met Ava thirty-one years ago."

"You want to keep your wife, but you want her to make room for the other women in your life. You won't leave other women alone, but you want to talk to your wife about what?"

Ron became annoyed by this ugly truth. The truth was he wanted his wife to continue being patient even after putting up with twenty-eight years of infidelity. Sherita made him realize he's not ready to end his infidelity yet…nor his marriage.

He tried to switch gears. "Well, what about this nation of greatness you mentioned? What's that about? Isn't that a good thing? That sounds wonderful."

"Take that deck of playing cards and shuffle, then shuffle the tarot cards again. The one card you pull from each will be your answer."

Again, Ron did as he was told. The playing card revealed the nine of hearts. Madame Juniót had already mentioned the nine a couple of times. The tarot card revealed the hangman again.

"Seems all roads lead to the same place for you."

"What does that nine mean? You keep saying it but won't explain what it is or this nation of greatness."

"I know the two are in the same. I just can't see what it is. You own a cat?"

"No. We have a sixteen-year-old dog who probably needs to be…" Ron had an epiphany. "Oh my God! The dog! They were talking about the dog needed to be put down. Why didn't I realize that last night before I fucked up again? Damn! How could I have been so fucking stupid?"

Madame Juniót nodded her head, letting him know he finally figured out how he had once again destroyed his marriage.

"And my wife said she wanted us to go away because it would be good for us. I said so many horrible things after that. I called her a liar. I was certain I heard them plotting, but now that I think about it, my eldest daughter, Shara, would call Fluffy a wildebeest because he's not a cute dog anymore. Damn! Damn! Damn! How could I have forgotten that?"

"The problem came before then. That conversation only gave you a clear path to the fool road you are hell-bent on traveling down."

"If I stay away from Sherita, will that fix everything in my marriage?"

"She's not going away. You have her soul inside of you, and there'll be plenty more souls you'll feel the need to collect, leaving no room for the center…your wife. Perhaps these souls have something to do with your great nation. Perhaps nine souls. Nine of hearts. That would make sense. I wondered if it was a cat and its nine lives. Things are typically very clear to

46

me until it comes to matters of the soul. That would explain why it's not made clear to me." Madame Juniót looked at her hourglass. "Your time is now up, but try to be mindful of doing foolish things from here on out. You already know it won't end well for you."

Ron chuckled. "Too late for that. I've been a fool for the past twenty-eight years."

"Agree!" Madame Juniót firmly stated. "But, you still have room to be a bigger fool, a much bigger fool."

"Thank you. I'll have to admit this has been rather insightful. I was expecting some sort of gimmick. You really are the real deal."

Once outside of the tent, she discreetly pointed in the direction of the other psychics. "They are gimmicks. Give people like me a bad rap."

"Is there a way to chat with you again if need be?"

"No. I flew from California for this event."

"I can fly to California to see you," Ron pleaded.

"No, I'd rather you don't. You suck a lot of energy, but may the spirits be with you and watch over you."

"Good spirits, I hope," Ron responded with an awkward chuckle.

Madame Juniót was already signaling for her next subject to sit in the chair to receive their sample reading, cueing Ron to move along. He waved as he walked away.

When he saw the usher, she asked, "Didn't I tell ya? Isn't she like the greatest?"

"I have to admit I was quite impressed, and I'm not an easy person to impress."

"Well, I'm glad you were pleased with your reading."

"Yes, I was. My momma's probably turning in her grave right now, but it was worth it. Anyhow, let me get on home and try to fix my broken scale."

"Great! Take care!" the usher said as she moved on to find more subjects for the psychics.

7

Ava quietly sat at her desk, staring at one of the computer screens inside her home office as Ron humbly entered.

"Hey, baby. You got a minute for us to talk about last night and everything?"

"Is there a point? Aren't you worried about me plotting to knock you off or something?"

Ron nervously chuckled as he fidgeted in his pockets.

"Yeah, I know. That sounds ridiculous hearing it now. That's what I want to discuss. I realized you were talking about putting our beloved Fluffy down since he's getting so old."

Ava's facial expression didn't change one bit. His lightheartedness didn't faze her.

"Anyhow, I owe you and the kids an apology."

"AGAIN?! Wouldn't you know it, but go ahead," she said as her eyes quickly darted from Ron to her computer screen, then back to Ron.

"Ava, I'm so sorry. I'm sorry for taking you for granted for so many years. I'm sorry that I haven't been a good husband and a father to our five beautiful children. I'm sorry for never supporting your dreams or career goals, and for being selfish by only wanting you to support mine or our children's. I'm sorry for expecting so much of you while always giving the bare minimum of myself. I'm sorry for all the lies and deception. I'm sorry for being pig-headed when you told me not to uproot the family and business to move to Atlanta. I'm even sorry for being jealous of the better relationship you have with my momma and family, as well as our children.

"Ava, what I'm trying to say is, it may have taken me a

long time to open my eyes finally, but they are wide open now, and I realize everything you are to me. You're my center. You are what makes my world revolve, and without my center, I'd be destroyed. I'd crash and burn. I need you. All I wanted to do yesterday was come home and have a night of passion with my beautiful wife, do anything I could to please you the way I used to do. Baby, I planned on coming in with the flowers and chocolates, pressing up behind you, wrapping my arms around your waist, and whispering in your ear how beautiful and sexy you are just to see your beautiful smile. Just like the one I see forming now. But then, I ended up hearing all that talk about killing, and you told the kids to hush before I came in and heard them. That made me bat-shit crazy at that moment.

"I read and listened to your text messages and voicemails only thirty-minutes ago, but I already knew I was on my way home to do whatever I had to do to help you understand my temporary insanity and to fix our marriage. And, yes, I think us taking a few days to go up to the mountains would be splendid. That's exactly what we need, and I'll be ready to go whenever you say let's go. I won't do like all those other times and put work first. As a matter of fact, we can take a trip to anywhere in the world. I can get Ariana to hold things down at the office."

Tears formed in Ava's eyes as she listened intensely to Ron's excessive speech. Her crooked smile made it difficult for him to tell if she was softening up or not buying a bit of what he was selling. However, Ron was shocked when Ariana's voice blared from the computer speakers.

"Momma, don't you dare fall for that bullshit again! Especially not after what I just told you."

"Tell Daddy to miss you with the bullshit!" Rashaun added.

Ron quickly rushed to the other side of one of her large desktop computer screens and saw Ava was on a video conference call with all five children, and during business hours at that. Ron knew that was indicative of a crisis. To have five directly-tied naysayers in his wife's ear spelled out what the tarot card spelled: D-E-A-T-H. He knew he was staring the death of his marriage in the face.

"What is this? Why didn't you tell me we weren't speaking in private?"

"I thought that apology was for the kids, as well. So what's the problem?" Ava asked very blasé with her hands folded.

"Could you disconnect that video call so I can speak with my wife in private, please?"

"Old man, you ain't got nothing else you need to be speaking to my mother about!" Jeremy said in an almost threatening tone.

"Yeah, and that goes double for me. Don't say shit else to my mother," Rashaun cosigned.

"And that goes triple, quadruple, double for me," Ariana added.

Shara sat quietly with her arms folded, but her expression screamed louder volumes than the other three combined.

"This is fucking insane. Daddy, you need to come to terms with reality. Y'all tried to make this shit work for way too long. Face it; it's over. You're over. You fucked up, and there's no coming back from this grave you've dug for this family. I hate this shit. I've always had your back, and you make me out to be the jackass each time I defend you. No more. Momma needs to find some self-respect and end this shit now before you damage us any worse than you already have," Eve expressed through heavy tears. "Daddy, you're done. You're over. Maybe one day in the future, you and I can have a father-daughter relationship again, but right now, I can't even see it happening. And your old ass already has one foot in the grave, so I'm not sure why you'd do such a stupid fucking thing now. All your other fuck-ups, and you do this shit now. Then you have the dastardly balls to be standing there bullshitting about how sorry you are and how you want to fix your marriage. Fuck off and fuck you, you lying bastard!" Eve disconnected from the video call.

"You go get that big house, talking about how you're getting it for the grandchildren. Newsflash! Nobody wants to bring children into this world with grandparents who are in a fucked-up, dysfunctional marriage and only staying together for the kids' sake. That's why we're not trying to have any. NONE! We don't want any of our children negatively influenced by a lying, cheating jackass like you. That's why you'll never hear the sound of baby feet pitter-pattering around in that stupid fucking house that you had to have, and probably because you thought these dumb girls out here would think you're a big shot. Well, guess what? You're not! You're a washed-up nobody. Maybe one of your hos will give you a baby so you can feel relevant again, but as soon as our mother finishes draining and dragging your nasty ass through the mud with this divorce, we'll be taking her back to Jersey where she can be happy with all of us together. Then you'll be left with nothing, not even that stupid house," Ariana finished with a slow roll of her neck before also disconnecting.

"My mother's ex-husband, all I'm going to say to you before I disconnect is you should've paid closer attention to the purchase orders Ariana signed off on. Then you might not have found yourself in this predicament." Shara laughed before disconnecting, as well.

"Man, fuck you and the air you breathe. I hope your dick falls off, 'cause you's a bitch anyhow," Rashaun said before he disconnected, too.

"Momma, I'll be on the next flight to come get you. Just say the word," Jeremy said.

Ava wiped her trickling tears and smiled. "I'll be fine. He's the one who'll be getting the fuck out of here until I'm ready to go. This is still my home until I say otherwise."

"So, we're not going to try to work on our marriage? You sat there and let me pour my heart out like a fool just to shut me down?"

"Nigga, you don't even have a heart. Kill that noise!" Jeremy laughed despite his anger.

Ron quickly reached for the keyboard and disconnected the call before Ava could stop him.

"Hey! Don't be touching my shit!" Ava yelled.

"We're married. It's community property just like this house. Now, what the hell is going on? Why are my kids showing such hatred towards me, more than they normally do? Yes, I thought I overheard you all plotting against me yesterday. But, I was mistaken and apologized for it."

"First of all, you need to back up and stop standing over me, making me feel threatened while I have this brass letter opener at my fingertips. Move!"

Ron raised his hands and backed away a few inches.

"So, you think your speech just made everything all well, huh?" Ava continued. "If I'm not mistaken, I believe I heard you say you were coming home last night to fuck me all night long. Isn't that what you said?" she asked, smiling.

Ron relaxed a little and smiled, as well. "Yes. Yes, I said that." He stepped nearer and took Ava's hands, pulling her from her seat. He stood pressed behind her and whispered, "You are so fucking beautiful and sexy. You have me so turned on right now. All I want to do is make love to the center of my universe," he said, trying to pull words from the psychic.

"Hmmm, that's a new one. Center of your universe, eh?"

"You sure are. Baby, I love you." He moved her long hair out of the way and began nuzzling the back of her neck and ear while groping her breasts.

Ava could feel herself weakening, but she knew their marriage had finally hit a point of no return.

"Sweetie, who's Lola?" she asked, already knowing.

He sincerely responded, "I don't know. Does she work for us?"

"Well, she called Ariana this morning and told her to check the tapes."

Confused, Ron stopped nuzzling.

"The tapes? What tapes? Here? The surveillance?"

"At the office."

"Oh, does she work in Accounting? Why would she bother Ariana about some tapes? That's not her job. We have CPAs for that stuff."

"No, dear, the videotapes," Ava politely answered before lowering the boom.

"What videotapes? Why would Ariana be bothered with videotapes? They have building security to monitor the outside premises."

"Yeah, I know that. I was talking about the interoffice video cameras that Ariana ordered a few months ago and just had installed a little over two months ago."

Puzzled and annoyed, Ron stepped away from Ava.

"That's a capital improvement. How did Ariana make such a purchase without my authorization?"

"Community property, remember? She didn't need your authorization as long as she had mine," Ava replied, her voice starting to lose its niceness.

"Okay, business property is not supposed to be community property, but whatever. What's the point?"

Ron was becoming equally tiresome of the dancing in circles.

"Anyhow, Ariana reviewed last night's videos right before you left the office to come home to fuck me–or quote-unquote make *LOVE* to me–all night long, and she was able to see you getting your dick cleaned by a clean-up woman. Fucking and sucking the bitch right there in your office with the door wide open, not giving a shit who saw. Then you ran straight home to fuck me, right? Oh, but close your mouth because it gets better. You had prearranged to meet the tacky bitch in a hotel this morning, and with all that community property shit going on, I was able to find the room you booked at the Marriott Gateway LAST NIGHT before your bitch-ass even made it home. And how convenient for you to come home and mistakenly overhear some bullshit plot to kill your ass, then use that as a reason for you to leave the house. Nah, you couldn't sleep in one of the other rooms of this eleven-bedroom house. Not sleep in the fully-furnished guesthouse. Not call the police about this supposed threat against your life. Not even a call to your fucking brothers or sister to tell them. Instead, you run to the presidential suite at the Marriott near the airport, which is over forty minutes away, rather than going to the Marriott that's only fifteen minutes away.

"BUT OHHHH! It gets even better. Just before you brought your black, crusty ass up in this house to pour out your heart, as you say, you had the audacity to extend the hotel reservation until Monday morning. You left the name of the clean-up woman, Sherita Walker, as a guest so she could pick up the room key at 2:17 this morning. And all this after your hearing some plot to kill you. Here's the biggest coincidence: the cleaning girl at our office happens to have that same name. Or should I say that bitch USED TO clean our offices. Because so help me, Ariana and I better not see her step foot in the parking lot. Then you added on a second room while you were extending the first reservation. More whores joining your party, huh?

"So, now, you go on. Run back to the dirty bitch you were planning on running back to AFTER you thought you were going to come up in here and fuck me. She can have you. Hell, I can still smell her pussy all over you, which tells me that you didn't even have the decency to brush your teeth or wash her scent off of you before trying to come in here thinking you were going to get straight to fucking me. This reminds me of when Rashaun was born. You came running to the hospital, wanting to kiss all over my newborn baby with your breath reeking of pussy. Nah, I had enough. Go and be her problem, because you won't be my problem anymore. We're done. This marriage is over; this conversation is done; and by the time I finish with your ass, that bitch won't get a dime."

Just as Ava was about to walk out of her office, she heard Ron mumble, "That's what this shit was about all along."

"What was what about?" Ava turned, demanding to know.

"MONEY! All you think about is how to get my fucking money. I'd give it all away to charity before I let you take anything I've built before even knowing you."

Ava laughed as she held up a finger, ready to lay him out.

"You know what? I'm not even going to waste my breath on your ass anymore. There's no need. You deserve everything you're about to get. All I have to do is sit back and enjoy the show. Go fuck your bitches. I don't even care anymore, but do know this. You have touched me for the last time. Now, I need to go find something to disinfect my neck and ear, you nasty bastard!"

Hesitantly, Ron was set to chase behind his wife, but his anger caused him to pause. When he finally did, he ran directly into Rashaun's fist instead.

"Stay the fuck away from my mother!" Rashaun yelled down at Ron, who had dropped to the floor.

Ava heard him and came running to grab her crying son, consoling him.

"You did this," Ava yelled at Ron.

Ron sat up stunned and in disbelief. He felt like he'd just got run over by a Mack truck. He couldn't believe his six-foot, four-inch, 225-pound son had punched him in the face. Rashaun's fist had caught his cheekbone. Ron could feel his heartbeat in that area from the heavy pulsation. It had quickly swelled. A part of him was afraid to say a word to Rashaun. Instead, he fumbled to get up from the floor. Rather than speak, he left home. He was still dizzy but felt it was best to get away from the heated moment.

Ron was so devastated by the day that he cried uncontrollably once inside of his car. He was angry at Ariana for ordering cameras without first discussing it with him instead of Ava. He was embarrassed that other people now had knowledge of his indiscretions there in the office. The thought of having to tell Sherita that she had been terminated from the job she so desperately needed saddened him, and all because he couldn't keep his hands to himself. He suddenly wondered if the installed camera had also captured his inappropriate phone conversations or visits to the porno sites on his office computer. Finally, he was amazed at how accurate the psychic had been about his crumbling life.

8

Ron watched from a distance as Sherita and several other young ladies splashed around in the swimming pool. They seemed to be having the time of their lives.

He checked his account at the hotel, fully expecting them to have racked up thousands of dollars in food and drinks by that point. To his surprise, Sherita had only ordered the cheapest items on the menu. The charges were for nine hamburgers at $8.95 each and several bottles of water.

Rather than let Sherita know he was back, Ron stayed holed up in the extra room, hiding his bruised face as well as his depression from losing his family. Sherita had texted him at least five times to let him know she missed him and hoped he was well. Also, she thanked him because her family was happy with his generous gift. Despite the storm in his life, her gratitude made him smile. He debated about the right time to let her know she had been terminated because of his deeds.

When his phone rang, he was glad to see it was his eldest brother, George, who had always been an ally for him.

"Aw, man, am I glad to hear from you," Ron answered.

"I don't know why, 'cause you should already know this isn't going to be a pleasant conversation. Man, what in the hell were you thinking? And then you got me stuck in the crossfire."

"How are you stuck in the crossfire, when this has nothing to do with you?"

"Now my wife of forty years thinks I'm on that same shit with you."

"Why would Linda think something like that? You're all

the way in Jersey."

"Doesn't matter. For all the years I've been working twelve to eighteen-hour days, she's now thinking I've been getting my freak on with the help like you."

"Aw, now that's not fair. In your defense, you own a very successful construction company that operates in eight different states, as well as in Mexico. Twelve to eighteen-hour days go with the territory. But, in my defense, people are making it like I've done this often. My wife was the first person who I have ever gotten involved with that was an employee of mine, and we've been together for thirty-one years and married for thirty. The other day is the only other time I've crossed the line with an employee. So, you need to let Linda know that I don't make it a habit of sleeping with my employees, and even if I did, it has nothing to do with your marriage."

"Ron, you know how close my Linda and your Ava are. And that's bullshit because you were doing some crazy girl when your baby boy was being born. He's only twenty-five. Every time you do stupid shit, Linda fusses at me as if I put you up to the shit. What would possess you to strike up an affair with the cleaning girl at your business? How'd that happen? You've had many, many, many women over the years, but they were professional women."

"Not all of them. Now that I think about it, most of them weren't professional women, because it was always the so-called professional women trying to stir up shit in my family. Like the dumb bitch did when Rashaun was born. They caused the most drama and had the most demands, always wanting me to leave my wife to be with them."

"Anyone ever tell you that you're a man-whore?" George laughed. "You are ridiculous. Forty years of marriage, and I have never cheated on Linda or even thought about it."

Ron was stunned by being called a man-whore two days in a row. "Funny you say that; I saw this psychic lady yesterday, and the first thing out of her mouth was her calling me a man-whore. I started to get up and walk away, but she actually dropped some jewels on me. I was impressed."

"A psychic? Ron, a psychic? Are you for real? You didn't need a psychic to tell you that you're a fuck-up. You knew that when you had that bitch on her knees, her head bobbing in your lap." George laughed.

"Whatever, man. I was trying to figure out what I needed to do to fix my marriage and my family."

"Perhaps you should have tried keeping your dick in your pants. I ain't no damn psychic, but I can tell you for free that shit is dead. D-E-A-D. Dead!" George laughed again. "Look, at this point, my only suggestion for you is to stay away without doing any extra stupid shit. Give it some time, and maybe one day, the two of you can at least have a cordial friendship. You're gonna need Ava again. Those young bitches are not going to be trying to change your soiled Depends. They're gonna move on to the next old dude with a few dollars. You are sixty-one years old. Sixty-two in a few months. Trust me, there have been those days when I think I have to pass gas, but poop shoots out of my ass instead. That's a fucked-up feeling. I ain't tell anyone about that shit other than my wife. She made me a doctor appointment, and they said that shit is normal for men when they get up in age. You think those young girls are going to be dealing with that shit? If you ain't giving them any reason to stay in your life, they're going to all bounce. Especially after your wife walks with everything."

That infuriated Ron. "My wife ain't getting shit. She's still young enough to go out and get a job. Hell, she devoted all of her time and energy to her kids. Let her go work for them," he said, pacing back and forth.

"Did you just really say that bullshit to me? Did you forget that I've been around from day one? Is that what you tell yourself to help you sleep at night? Did you call them 'her kids' as if your sperm didn't create at least four of them? Man, you're really on some whole other shit."

"Her son punched me in my face yesterday, and as far as I'm concerned, he is not my child. My child would never strike his father." Ron stopped in front of the mirror, examining his bruise as he spoke.

"They thought you were hurting Ava when you disconnected the video call. Jeremy couldn't get there, so he asked Rashaun to go and check on their mother. Rashaun saw his mother running away from his father, and instincts kicked in. Can you blame him? We would have done the same if it were our mother. Well, at least I would have."

"Hell yeah, I blame him. He's a child and needs to stay in a child's place."

"No, he's a twenty-five-year-old man who needs to look after his momma."

"Whatever! They can have each other. Every last one of them is disrespectful toward me. They talk about killing me, wishing I would drop dead, and taking everything from me like they're entitled to the fruits of all my hard work."

"Ron, so you're going to sit there and run that bullshit that your wife didn't help your company to have the huge success it has right now, while giving birth and raising all of your children—even Shara, who you wanted no parts of—while you were out screwing anything you thought would have a tighter pussy than the one that had to open wide enough to bear your fucking children? You're not going to try to run that bullshit to me, right?"

"My company was already successful when I met Ava, who was a mail clerk for *my* successful company."

"Now, fast-forward to how your company was about to go under a few months after meeting your mail clerk, Ava. She wrote up a whole bunch of business development ideas, even looked at your finances and asked the questions that led to you learning you were being robbed by several of your highly-educated white-collar employees. You put her ideas into play, promoted her to Business Development Manager, and ended up marrying her a couple of months later."

Ron sucked his teeth. "Man, you calling me just to get under my skin. I thought you were going to be a friendly ear, an ally."

"What am I supposed to ally? You threw away your family, always taking up with a bunch of young, dumb bitches who'll probably try to get pregnant so they can move into your house and let you take care of them. Oh, and I'm sure your company will be plagued with scandals of you forcing employees to have sex with you to keep their jobs."

"I have never done that!"

"Prove you didn't."

"How am I supposed to prove I didn't?"

"That's my point. You can't. All they'll need to know is that's how you started with your wife, did your wife while she was giving birth, and how you finished with your wife— sleeping with an employee. And from what I understand from watching that video, the girl didn't seem to have much of an option. If she didn't do what you told her, would she have kept her job? Somehow, I doubt she would have, which would give people the impression that you force yourself on your employees."

Ron was disgusted with himself and ready to cry. In the back of his mind, Ron knew he would have booted Sherita out of his company had she denied his requests, but he would never admit it to anyone, not even his brother. Talking to his brother only made him feel worse. Suicide crossed his mind, but the thought of his children inheriting a dime troubled him.

"How do I fix things with my wife? That's the only thing I need to know."

"Ron, that's done. I know you don't want to hear that, but you've cheated almost the entire time while married to a beautiful, solid woman who stuck by you through nearly thirty years of infidelity. Through everything you have thrown her way, she hung in there, only to be treated like shit time and time again. Two months ago, you even made a promise to me that you were done cheating. You licked and screwed some random bitch who you knew nothing about, then tried to go home to fuck your wife. All while planning to go fuck the random bitch when you finished fucking your wife. Worse, your wife got to see the video of you fucking this chick with no protection only minutes after meeting her. I can't help but wonder how many diseases you've given your wife that neither of you has ever admitted to anyone.

"My brother, what do you think you can fix? You ain't ever gonna change. You were a dog long before you got married. Shocked the hell out of me that you would ever marry, and the fact that you would even lie to me just two months ago, saying you were done cheating, tells me that you'll never change. But, tell me this. What made you choose that girl on that night? Was she someone you had been checking out before and couldn't stop thinking about?"

"No. I don't remember ever seeing her before that night. I was in my office earlier that evening checking out a new online porno site, all the while thinking of ways to excite my wife later that night. I was actually anxious to get home to Ava, because when we're good, we're really good. Later, I stepped out to go drop some files off to Accounting and then headed to the men's room. I was planning on going back to my office and packing up to go straight home. On the way back, I overheard these girls talking, and one of them mentioned she likes dealing with older men. I saw her playfully pat her ass, and instantly, I wanted her. That's it. Hell, I didn't even realize how pretty she was until she came to see me at the hotel. She's fine as hell. Crazy thing is, I couldn't fuck her that night at my office because I couldn't stop thinking about how much I love–and preferred to be with–my wife. That's why I was determined to go home and fix my marriage."

"You say that, but booked extra nights to be with her in the hotel after. That makes no sense."

"Okay, fuck it! Yes, I like her. Yes, I might want to be with her. Yes, I want my wife, and I want the side piece, too. No, I'm not trying to make this girl my wife. Now you have the total truth. And yes, I will continue to see her until I decide I'm done with her. I extended the hotel reservation so she could invite her friends and family to hang out with her for the weekend. I thought I'd be home with my wife. I booked an extra room just in case things didn't work out at home, and I've been in this room since yesterday by myself. I saw her having fun at the pool with some other girls, and I didn't want to bother her. However, looking at the other girls made me realize even more that I couldn't settle down with her."

"And why is that?" George asked.

"Because I wanted to fuck the other girls, as well. They were all fine and sexy as hell. Beautiful bodies. I'm talking pussy for days on end."

"Just a couple of minutes ago, your sad-sounding self was asking how to fix your marriage and talking about how you prefer your wife. Now you're telling me about how you've been thinking about fucking a whole harem of young girls all at once. Does that not sound insane to you?"

Ron was now excited over his lustful thoughts. "Bro, I'm trying to tell you, they had ass, tits, flat bellies, sexy thighs, nice hair…none of that weave shit. Hell, you're the one saying my marriage is over. My wife said it's over. So, fuck it. I'm trying to lick my wounds and move on."

"And what are you going to do when they turn up pregnant since you don't concern yourself with protection?"

"I have an eleven-bedroom house. They can come live with me. You know what? You just gave me a good idea. I think I'll move them into my home and fuck any of them whenever I feel like it." Ron laughed.

"Don't be blaming me for your stupid thoughts. I want no parts of that idea because now I know you have officially gone insane. I don't think you can just move your mistresses into your wife's home."

"My wife's home?! I bought that house."

"I don't have anything else to say. You are too stupid."

"No, I'd be stupid if I sit around pining away over a woman who doesn't want to be with me anymore. She wants to move on, said for me to go on with my bitches. Then that's what I'm going to do. I got plenty of money, and I got a big piece of meat that still works very well and that the ladies love. Instead of me sitting cooped up in this hotel room watching porn on my laptop, I see a whole bunch of fine, young specimens that'll give me whatever I want when I want it." Ron laughed. "You know what that psychic lady said? She said something about I'm going to have a great new nation, and she even mentioned the number nine. There are nine plump asses for me to stick my shit into, and who knows, if a kid or two comes out of the deal, I can make sure those other ungrateful asshole children of mine won't see a dime of my money if I ever die."

"What the fuck?! Did that psychic lady tell you how that stupid shit is going to work out for you? That sounds like some scam bullshit, telling you about some great new nation."

"She showed me a hangman card and said it wouldn't end well, but at this point, I don't give a fuck. I'm now a free man, and I'm going to enjoy my freedom and all the fruit that comes along with it. No more sneaking, lying, or hiding. When Ava realizes that guys aren't banging down her door to do more than 'wham, bam, thank you ma'am', she'll be begging for me to take her ass back."

"Okay, now that's really crazy. I gotta go. You need help. Professional help. I can't help you, and it doesn't seem like your psychic lady helped you either. You're a damn fool. I love you, but you're on your own, bro. I called hoping to talk some sense into you."

"Hey, well then, let me go get this crazy party started then. I'm done crying over spilled milk."

"We'll talk soon. I'm sure there'll be plenty of updates."

After ending the call, Ron took a little time to map out his game plan to see how he could succeed in accomplishing his ultimate goal. He knew it might be upsetting to Sherita. However, the way he saw it, since she was now jobless, she had little choice but to go along with whatever he wanted, how he wanted, and when he wanted. Ron fondled himself with a broad grin as he thought of having sex with each of the ladies, and even better, being able to control them.

9INE

At nine o'clock that night, the limo picked up the nine ladies that would share a festive night on the town with Ron. Wanting to give the women a taste of what he was offering, he had loads of cash.

The ladies were beside themselves. The only party limo they had seen the inside of was on television. Ron stood outside of the limo and greeted each with a warm hug as they entered. This was the first time he was seeing each of the women up close, and his struggle at that moment was trying to decide which one he would fuck first. He knew he still had unfinished business with Sherita, but since he already knew what she felt like, she wouldn't be his first choice.

To Ron, their outfits were tasteless, but with them being economically disadvantaged, he figured it was their finest clothes. Aside from their attire being tacky, it was very appealing just the same. He found himself turned on by each.

"Okay, so can I get an introduction of all the beautiful ladies in my company?" he asked once they were seated and on their way.

The ladies were giddy and anxious to get drinks from the bar.

Sherita decided to make the introductions. "Ron Johnson, this is my youngest sister, Sherrell. She's the one who I told is eighteen, so I don't know why she's reaching for the vodka."

Everyone laughed.

"This is my middle sister, Shirleen. She's twenty and ain't got no business pouring that Henny."

Again, they all laughed. Shirleen stuck up a middle finger

at Sherita.

"Over here is my cousin, Tonjenae. Most of the times we call her Tonji."

"Yeah, and I'm legal! I'm twenty-one," Tonjenae said, holding up a drink she had poured herself.

Sherita continued, "That's Toni, Tonjenae's younger sister, but they are both like our sisters since we all live together with my mother. And these are some of their friends."

Everyone else waved.

"I'm Sherrell's friend, Kennedy, and this is my older sister, Kendra.

"Kendra is like my best friend ever, and I was always at their house. Their momma is like my play momma. Kendra's definitely my ride or die."

"What's your name? I don't think I caught it," Ron asked, enthralled by the excessive cleavage exposed on her petite five-foot frame.

"Oh, I'm Angela."

"I guess that leaves me. I'm Erica. I used to work as a store clerk with my girl, Toni, but probably got fired since we didn't show up for work today. I'm the bougie one of the bunch, and I'm the champagne drinker and thinker."

Everyone laughed, while Ron just smiled.

"So, you drink champagne often?" he asked, captivated by her golden eyes.

"Shoot no!" Sherita answered. "She tasted champagne for the first time when she got to the room and had some from that bottle."

Ron frowned. "That was probably flat since it was sitting opened. We'll have to see about getting you some fresh champagne. Matter of fact, there should be a fresh bottle in the minibar right there."

"I saw a few small bottles of champagne underneath." Kendra bent to check, taking Ron's breath away. "See, here," she said, handing a bottle to Erica.

Erica didn't know how to remove the foil wrapping. So, Ron reached for the bottle and took care of it, along with pouring a glass for her. Erica's eyes were undoubtedly flirting as she took the drink from him. Realizing Sherita didn't have anything, he offered her a glass of champagne, as well. She was somewhat in her feelings and feeling neglected by Ron as she watched him be attentive to the ladies, but she felt she wasn't in a position to complain.

When they arrived at the Steak House, a well-known hangout for celebrities, they were beside themselves. Ron watched from the sidelines as they struggled to keep their micro-mini dresses and skirts from exposing their assets. Every head turned as the women strutted in their six-inch heels to a private dining room already set up for them. They looked like a bunch of teenagers pretending to be grown-ups, especially with their poor application of makeup. Ron didn't know if he should look proud to be flanked by the nine beauties, or embarrassed since they were barely of legal, consenting age...despite their womanly bodies.

He purposefully chose not to sit next to or across from Sherita. He didn't want her treating the outing as if they were a couple or as if they were exclusive. He didn't want to sit at the head of the table either. Instead, he sat Sherita on one end and Erica on the other end. He purposely sat directly across from Angela since she had to repeatedly cover her areola, which turned him on as he envisioned her massaging his dick between her breasts.

"Can we order anything?" Angela asked. "There's no prices on the menu."

Before Ron could look up from his menu to answer, Sherita's youngest sister, Sherrell, burst out laughing and said, "Angela, your titty is out."

Kendra laughed. "Well, that was the point of a low-cut dress."

Angela high-fived her, as they seemed to do often, and then

fixed the material back over her bosom.

"Well, Mr. Ron, I hope you've seen titties before, because I swear this damn dress is acting up. I done fixed it over and over. Shoot, if I show a titty or two, I might be able to order some of everything."

Angela laughed and high-fived Kendra once more, causing her areola to become visible again.

Ron chuckled, somewhat embarrassed. "You ladies are welcomed to order whatever and as much as you'd like."

Out the corner of his eye, he could see Sherita shooting daggers at Angela. Ron's eyes returned to his menu, although he knew what he wanted without looking.

"So what happened to your face? It looks like someone hit you," Erica asked.

"A bit of family drama. Not a big deal."

"You hit your wife?" Erica continued to probe.

Ron was stunned by the question. "No! Not at all. I've never hit a woman in my life. Truthfully, it was my son. My family's a bit angry about me providing you all with this experience," he lied, hoping to gain their sympathies.

"Oh, that's fucked up," Sherrell commented as she placed her hand on Ron's thigh as he had hoped when he created the seating arrangement. "I'm sorry you had to go through that to show us a nice time. This is like the best time of my life,"

"I'm sorry for being all nosey, up in your business like that. I'm thankful for everything you've done for us, and I really appreciate you," Erica flirtatiously added with a smile and licking the lip gloss from her top lip.

Ron could feel his blood flowing down to the head of his tool. Erica's deliciously thick lips made him forget there were other women seated at the table.

"Oh my goodness, who got hit?" Angela asked when she caught onto the conversation.

Ron looked to Angela and her exposed nipple again.

Sherrell tried to point it out using a hand gesture, but

Angela responded with, "Fuck it!"

As the evening progressed, Shirleen, Sherita, and Tonjenae excluded themselves from most of the conversations, which were oftentimes blatantly flirtatious. Erica even asked what was the most women he'd been with at the same time. Ron just chuckled at their banter.

"Mr. Ron, wouldn't you love these thick, luscious lips on your dick? Hell, I'll go underneath the table right now so you won't have to wait for it," Erica said, daring Ron with her invitation.

Kendra laughed. "And she's the one who calls herself bougie. That ain't what classy people do."

Ron wanted to tell Kendra to mind her business.

However, Kendra offered up her own contribution. "But I got the best ass out of the bunch, and a lot more can be done with it. And I know how to make it clap. These bitches be wanting me to teach them."

"I don't know about y'all, but I'm ready to go. My pussy is wetter than a motherfucker," Angela said.

"Same here," Erica added.

"I hope you got one of those pills to keep you going, because it seems you're gonna have some heavy-duty work to do tonight," Kennedy voiced, surprising Ron with her bluntness.

"Wow!" Ron said. He couldn't remember ever having such an intriguing conversation in his life. He didn't even realize when Sherita rose from the table and walked up behind him.

"What's going on down here?" she asked with a smile while seething inside.

"Girl, we trying to hurry up and get the hell up out of here so we can get a piece of that big dick," Erica informed her. She figured she was upsetting Sherita since she knew Sherita thought Ron was going to be her man.

"I'm definitely ready to go," Sherrell said.

Sherita was annoyingly surprised. "Oh wow! My baby

sister? Didn't expect that."

"Girl, please, you're the one always hollering about some nine-to-one ration of women to men. Well, we are nine beautiful, sexy women with one man who has a fat dick that I want to feel inside me," Sherrell responded, rubbing Ron's crotch.

"Alrighty! Anyhow, I'm going to the ladies' room. Anyone care to join me?" Sherita asked as she fought back her tears.

No one budged, and Ron refused to be moved by Sherita's emotions. As far as he was concerned, if she didn't like what was about to go down, she was welcomed to hop back in her car and head back to Griffin.

After Sherita walked away, Tonjenae got up and stood near her sister, while Shirleen stood near Sherrell.

"What's wrong with Sherita? She looked like she was about to cry," Tonjenae asked.

"I think she thought someone at this table was her man but found out he's not," Erica answered, amused. "Hell, we 'bout to head back to the hotel and find out what he's working with."

"I wanna know if he's skilled enough to handle all this natural, unenhanced ass," Kendra said, patting the side of her behind when she stood up.

"Damn, that's cold," Tonjenae laughed, "but I definitely wanna watch."

"I wanna watch, too," Shirleen said. "Beats watching porno. So, why are we still sitting here? We need to box all this shit to go."

"Come here and feel this. Then tell me if all you wanna do is watch," Sherrell told her sister.

Shirleen and Tonjenae both reached in for a feel as Ron allowed the ladies to have their way.

"Shoot! My cycle just started this morning. So, I don't have a choice but to sit this one out. Hopefully, there will be a next time."

"Damn! That's fucked up," Kendra said.

Ron couldn't believe how smoothly things were going. At first, he wasn't sure how he was going to seduce them all to be on board, but as it turned out, they did the seducing.

He summoned for the server to collect their food and box it up for those who wanted it for later. Sherita was still in her feelings, and Ron was still unbothered by them.

When they were back in the limo, the women wasted no time seducing Ron and giving him lap dances. Sherita sat off in the corner of the limo watching as her blood boiled from jealousy. In minutes, the ladies had his pants open and his dick standing to attention. Angela had her breasts out and trying to feed him a hardened nipple. Kendra placed one of his hands in between her thick thighs so he could feel her wetness. Erica quickly cornered the market by administering the blow job her lips promised in the restaurant. The others tried to get a touch or feel in where they could. By the time they made it back to the hotel, Ron had orgasmed from Erica's blowjob; Kendra had an orgasm from him finger fucking her; and Angela had an orgasm from Kendra's fingers. They pulled themselves together to head into the hotel.

As they headed towards the elevators, everyone was excited except for Sherita. It was clear to anyone watching that there was about to be a major fuck fest. When the elevator doors opened in the lobby, a familiar face greeted Ron.

"Hey, Mister Johnson. Hey, Sherita."

It was an employee from his office.

"Hello," Ron nervously replied.

"There's a bunch of us over near the bar. You should come over and say hello."

That was the last thing Ron wanted, and he hated that the employee recognized Sherita.

"No, dear, we got a party to get to with the quickness," Kendra said, pushing her breasts against Ron's back, causing him to move forward into the awaiting elevator.

The other ladies quickly crowded in, laughing and

giggling. Not amused, Sherita just waved with a somber face, as if she didn't want to be there. The employee looked concerned as the elevator doors closed.

When the elevator doors opened to their floor, Ron decided to change the plans. He didn't want Sherita in his face, and he didn't want to think about the flack he would have to deal with once back in the office.

"I know you ladies are looking to spend some time together, but there's going to be a little change in plan."

The ladies expressed their disappointment.

"Don't worry. I'll see each of you. But, for right now, I'm going to take Erica, Kendra, and Angela back to my room with me, and of course, Tonjenae to watch."

The chosen ladies were beyond excited. The others were sorely disappointed.

"Y'all bitches may as well go on to bed because we gonna be rocking the hell out of this shit tonight. He ain't gonna have any energy left for y'all," Kendra bragged as she twerked.

"I promise I won't send you home disappointed," Ron tried to assure them. "In the meantime, order whatever you want from room service."

"Ron, can I speak with you a minute in private?" Sherita asked, obviously disturbed.

"Sorry, it'll have to wait until later," he callously replied.

His response pissed her off even more, and she walked on to her suite door and went inside. The others not chosen followed her lead. The chosen ladies happily followed him to his suite. Once inside, he ordered a few items from room service. The ladies were already stripping naked, and by the time he hung up the phone, they were stripping off his clothes, as well.

There was a method to his selection. With the delightful sight of her full ass on her five-foot-three-inch frame with a slender waist and voluptuous breasts, and after feeling deep inside of Kendra, he couldn't wait for his dick to be up inside her along with being smothered by her tits. He wanted to fuck Kendra as he watched Kendra pleasure Angela and vice versa. He definitely couldn't wait to squeeze in between Angela's extra-large boobs, which sat at full attention on her petite five-foot frame. With Erica, there was something special about her golden-brown eyes, naturally golden-blonde hair, and flawless golden-brown complexion that captured him from their introduction, along with her succulent thick lips. He looked forward to returning the favor she gave him in the limo. Not only that, he wanted to make passionate love to the five-foot-four sun goddess. He felt a deep connection. Although Tonjenae was there as a spectator, he was going to allow her to suck his dick and see how she compared to Erica. She was the tallest of all the ladies, standing around five-foot-ten, and he had already imagined banging her up against a wall one day, with her long, shapely legs wrapped around him.

He moved the other ladies away from him to grab hold of Tonjenae. He released her braless breasts from her camisole top and sucked each one.

"I can't," she whispered. "I'm on my period."

"I know. I have something else for you to do," he whispered back.

He sat on the bed and guided her head down. Tonjenae was hesitant but went for it. He lied on his back and summoned Erica to climb onto his face. That excited Kendra and Angela, who helped out by kissing, sucking, and caressing Erica's breasts, as well as stimulating her clit. Ron was glad for the assistance because, from time to time, Tonjenae's superior skills made him forget what he was supposed to be doing. She was more skilled than Sherita and even better than Erica, he had to admit.

Tonjenae sucked the explosion from his volcano. Neither Erica or Tonjenae acted squeamish about swallowing, and that delighted him.

Timing was perfect because room service knocked with the

delivery of fruit, chocolate-covered strawberries, champagne, cranberry juice, sodas, water, ice cream, cookies, and chocolate syrup.

"Uh-oh! Looks like shit's about to get all the way live up in this mother!" Tonjenae laughed.

"I aim to please," Ron said.

"You do indeed," Erica told him. "My pussy is still over here talking about that tongue lashing. A good damn tongue lashing."

I can't wait to ride that dick, Kendra added"

"Yes!" Erica agreed.

Ron used a hand to play in Kendra's pussy. She lifted a knee to allow Ron deeper access inside of her. Ron's dick jerked like crazy while watching Angela perform cunnilingus on Erica like an expert. Erica, being the unselfish one, decided to flip around into a sixty-nine position with Angela. Whenever Tonjenae wasn't sucking Kendra's breasts, she and Kendra would passionately kiss.

Ron wasn't sure how much more he could take. He was ready for his dick to blow a hole into someone's young pussy. Although Ron had planned for Erica to be first, he didn't dare break up what she had going ferociously with Angela. Kendra was closer and easier access, so he slid into her home base. Talk about being a team player; Tonjenae positioned herself to kiss Kendra while inserting fingers into Erica. Eventually, Ron decided to do Kendra one-on-one and flipped her over so she could display her skills. She had Ron working up a serious sweat and earned every bit of the nut he busted inside of her. As Kendra lay spent against Ron's chest while on the chair the pair ended up moving to, the other ladies lay drained on the bed.

"I want to get some more of this," Ron whispered for only Kendra to hear. "Lots more. Make sure we keep in touch. Will you do that?"

"Hell yeah," she answered.

"I guess I better go take care of Angela before I get too relaxed."

"Yeah, I guess. We might have to suck it to get it back up again. What you think?"

Ron kissed Kendra before getting up. Then he walked over to the trays left by room service to eat some fruit and gulp down a bottle of water.

"Come on, Angela. You're up next. We gotta get him up again," Kendra said.

"Heyyy! That works for me," Angela said, anticipating her turn to show Ron what she could do.

Ron started with pulling Angela to him for a Swedish massage. He felt she was unskilled in that area but trainable. Afterward, he laid on the bed while Kendra and Angela went to work on him. When he was hard enough, Angela climbed onto his dick. Ron couldn't believe how super tight her pussy was on his dick; he wasn't expecting such tightness. He got up and flipped Angela on her back. He fucked her small frame like a ragdoll. He knew he was hurting her and got a thrill from watching the pain on her face. Her body kept trying to escape the pounding he was inflicting, but he kept pulling her back to him.

"Damn, he's a fucking beast," Tonjenae said, impressed with Ron's powerful performance. "Looks like he's putting a serious beating on her ass."

"Shit, I thought we were doing something," Kendra said, equally surprised. "Erica, I can't imagine him having anything left for you after that."

"Nah, he's saving his best performance till the end. See, he and I have chemistry. We'll have a powerful climax together. We'll make love, not just fuck. He sees me as more than just a fuck. I be knowing these things," Erica bragged.

"Yeah right!" Kendra laughed.

Ron turned Angela's body in all kinds of angles until he finally came. To Angela, that pounding felt like forever. It felt good, but it was equally as painful. She wasn't sure if she could handle another round with him.

"That was a damn good fucking to watch," Tonjenae commented when Ron returned from the bathroom.

"I'm almost jealous," Kendra said, chuckling.

"Ladies, unfortunately, I'm going to have to call it a night. The other ladies will have to wait until tomorrow. I'm about to hop in the shower–"

"I told you he was going to be too tired for your ass," Kendra said as she laughed to Erica.

"As I was saying, I'm about to hop in the shower, and I'd like for Erica to join me, alone. You ladies can return to your room."

Erica cheesed extra hard at Kendra. "What? What was that you were saying? I can't hear you."

Angela and Kendra put their clothes on and left with Tonjenae. After they were gone, Ron told Erica, "I changed my mind. I want to fix a nice bath for us and have some champagne. How does that sound to you?"

She walked over and kissed him as if he were her man. He was *really* feeling Erica.

While they were relaxing together in the tub, he confessed, "I want to make love to you. I don't know what it is about you. Probably those hypnotic, golden eyes you have. You stood out from the others. I knew I wanted to spend the whole night with your bougie ass." He laughed. "Hell, I can even see you living in my house with me and driving my cars. That's why I set you at the head of the table. You look regal, like you belong there, but I need you to know, I am incapable of being with just one woman, but I'd make you my number one lady."

"It all sounds good, but you got Sherita over there thinking she's your lady and then you got a wife. How's that all supposed to work out?" she asked before taking a sip of her champagne.

"I don't know. This is all new to me. My wife said it's over, so it's over. Fuck it! I'm moving on, and I like what I've found. As for Sherita, I never gave her the impression that we were exclusive. I saw her; I was horny; I wanted to fuck her, and I did…or at least I tried to but never finished. I just feel like she's unfinished business."

"So, if I'm with you, I have to be okay with sharing you with the others?"

"Probably. The others, I could take them or leave them, but still, you'd be number one."

"We live way in Griffin. How are we supposed to see each other? My place is super small."

"I'm going to figure out a way to move you into my house."

"Oh really?! I thought you were just saying that."

"No, I'm very serious."

"So, what if I'm not okay with sharing you? What if I fall madly in love and want you all to myself?"

"Unfortunately, you're going to have to share me if you want to be with me. My wife had to share me almost our entire marriage. She was my number one, but now she decided she doesn't want that anymore."

"Why? What changed?"

"It's kind of complicated. My kids found out about Sherita then got into my wife's head, and that was it."

"That's how you got the bruise on your face?"

"Yep! My son."

"What are your kids gonna say if I move into your house?"

"They said they're done with me, so they don't have shit to say."

"You know what? If you still feel the same way in a few weeks or a month, and you're sure about ending things with your wife, then I'll say yes."

"That sounds fair. I knew you were as intelligent as you are beautiful."

Erica turned around in the large tub to sit facing Ron. She kissed him. She wanted him to love her enough that he'd move her into that number one spot in his home and his life.

After a night of passion, Ron was determined to find a way to move Erica into his home. She's the one who he wanted to wake up to in the mornings if it wasn't going to be Ava.

10

Ron managed to have a go with all of the ladies before they checked out that Monday morning. Sherita wasn't too thrilled when she learned she no longer had a job. Ron offered to continue paying her a salary while she looked for employment.

When he tried having sex with Sherita again, she made it feel more like a chore, and particularly since Erica made it immediately known that she was going to be Ron's number one.

He worked in another round with just Erica and Kendra present. They had two distinct sexual styles, and he loved them both. Trying to one-up Erica, who she clearly didn't like, Kendra told Ron that she wanted to one day try anal sex. He was hoping Erica would also suggest it, but she didn't. So, before dismissing the ladies with the three hundred dollars each that he'd given them, he decided to take Kendra up on her backdoor offer, utilizing Angela in a sixty-nine position with Kendra. That was by far the perfect ending to Ron's glorious weekend.

*****

Ron went home Monday afternoon prepared to do battle. He planned on letting Ava know that he was moving his new lady into HIS home.

Ava laughed hysterically. "Oh, you think?"

"No, I don't think. I am. I'm being courteous by giving you a heads up."

"You want to be with your bitch, then go find a place for

you and her, because she damn sure isn't coming up in my home where I live."

"She *will* be coming to live with me in *my* home."

"You must want your kids to go to jail for beating the bitch down. To go along with something so stupid, she must be younger than your youngest child. Probably just a hiccup older than our twelve-year-old granddaughter," Ava said, shaking her head.

"Doesn't matter how old she is. She's coming, and no one's going to touch her. I'll have all of your disrespectful children locked up if they touch her or ever touch me again."

"You have the nerve to call someone else disrespectful, when you're trying to bring your mistress to live in my home."

"You said we're done, didn't you? So, I'm respecting your wishes and moving the fuck on with my life."

"And since it's my home, I'll have the bitch put the fuck out, and there ain't a damn thing you can do about it."

"Oh, that's what you think? Well, I should have started with telling you that she's having my baby. Therefore, she has every right to live in my home with me if I want her to," he fabricated. "Call your attorney if you want. They'll tell you."

The look on Ava's face made him think he better stop trying to push her buttons.

"You got Sherita pregnant? That would mean you've been fucking her long before Thursday."

"Sherita? Heck no! Her name is Erica, and I love her."

Ava closed her eyes as a deranged smile formed on her lips. "You love her? You were just begging to fix our marriage like two or three days ago, and now you want to tell me that you got one of your hos pregnant and you love the bitch?" She laughed and shook her head. "Man, if you don't get your silly ass the fuck up out of my face with your shit, I swear to God that I will stab your black ass, and I'll stab that ho if you ever bring her up in my face."

"Ava, you can say what you want. I understand that this is

hurtful to you, but it's time for us to move on with our lives. We both know we haven't been happy for years. Now I'm ready to be happy, just without you."

Shaken, Ava had to take a seat. Ron rushed to her aid.

"Get the fuck away from me, you sick bastard! You selfish motherfucker!"

"I'm selfish for wanting to be happy? Tell me, were you happy in this thirty-year marriage whereas I was only faithful for the first two years?"

For the first time, Ron's insanity made sense to Ava, but it still seemed so unfair to her. He was happy ALL thirty years. She was the miserable one. She was the one who put her happiness aside for everyone else. She had no words left to say, so she cried. He tried to console her, but she pushed him away and walked into the next room.

He hated what he was doing, but at the same time, he realized he was helping his wife by pushing her out of his life. There's no denying that he loved her more than life itself and would until the day he died, but it didn't mean they belonged together. He doesn't know the reason for his sick obsession with eighteen and nineteen-year-old girls, but he knew it was a problem that existed before he met his wife. She was only nineteen when they met, and he was already thirty. Perhaps Ava had just gotten too old for his standards. Thirty years later, and he was still fixated on eighteen and nineteen-year-old women.

He figured he'd talk about the probability of moving Erica and even Kendra in at another time, when she had been able to process the fact that the divorce was inevitable. The thought of waking up with Erica and Kendra every day gave him an incredible feeling. He became aroused. Anxious to play out his plans, Ron went to look through the rooms to decide on a suitable one for the ladies.

"I wanted to believe you were only saying what you said to try to hurt me for some unknown reason, but I see you happily preparing a place for her. Now I know you were being honest," Ava said when she found him going from room to room.

Ron stood for a moment, debating if he should be candid since she seemed to be civil.

"I haven't been completely honest," he told her.

"So you're not bringing your mistress here to live? You were just trying to hurt me?"

He closed his eyes and took a deep breath before answering. "No, I didn't say it to hurt you, and yes, they–"

"They?!"

"Yes, there is more than one. They will be coming here to live with me. It's what I want. Right now, they are who I want. I know you're not trying to hear this, but I really do love you and always will. You deserve better than what I have given you. Everything that happened in the past few days needed to happen. It was like an infected abscess that finally needed to burst. Now everything's out in the open. Honestly, I wish I could still have you in my life as my wife, but I know with the kids in your ear, we will never have the peace we'd need to keep our marriage going."

Ava looked confused. "Uh, when you say you want to have me in your life as your wife still, are you suggesting we stay married, sleep in the same bed, but that I have to share you with others knowingly?"

Ron shrugged. "I don't know. I guess that's what I'm saying. I don't want to lose you, especially when I know they're only a fad that I'll lose interest in soon. Eventually, I'm not going to want to be with them, just like all the rest. But, I always end up with my heart in my hands and extending it to you."

"You just told me you love this girl and want her to move into my home. That sounds like more than a fad. You didn't do that with the others."

Again, he shrugged. "I'm sorry. The truth is, I just met her, but I knew from first sight that she wasn't going to be a simple fly-by-night romance. I honestly never felt like this towards any of the others. The only other time in my life I've felt this way was when I met you. Things were different back then compared to now. I'm ready to settle down, have more fun in my life, probably travel more, and step away from the business."

"Despite me waiting thirty years for you to get to this point where we could do all those things together, now you want to do it with little girls who are straight out of high school, if that?"

"I'm sorry. I want what I want."

Ava shook her head and walked away into their bedroom. She didn't know what to do anymore. It was one thing to share her husband as long as he kept his behaviors discrete…at least for the most part. It was something else to move his lovers into her home and sex them under her nose. She didn't want her marriage to be over, and if the kids didn't know about the Sherita affair, she would have still been willing to stick with him. However, with the kids now involved, she'd lose not only the respect of her children but the relationship with them, as well. They'd want nothing more to do with her as well as their father. That thought alone made her decision easier.

She turned from the window she was gazing out of and found him in the doorway watching her with a look of love and adoration.

"I will say this one thing; if you bring anyone into my home to live, visit, or to even fuck, consider that a declaration of war. That I promise you. You are not ready for that, and you most certainly will not win."

Not expecting that response, he was stunned. He thought for sure she'd see things his way and be willing to save their marriage while allowing him to have live-in side pieces.

"Well, consider this war then," he said before turning to walk out of the room and the house.

That made her nervous, but she was determined not to give

in to his selfish arrangement that benefitted her in no way. She didn't feel up for a fight, but she was left with little choice. The one thing that made her laugh about the situation was that Ron, like always, failed to recall she held all of the power to his business, his finances, the house, the kids. EVERYTHING.

11

Ron was ready to set his big idea in motion. Two weeks had gone by, and everything had been quiet on the home front. At the office, there had been gossiping about him being with several women at a hotel. The whispers were disturbing enough to keep Ariana away from the office. He would be sure to have the video feed removed from his office, but not before inviting Kendra up to give a rousing performance.

He invited the nine women to meet him in one of the conference rooms at the hotel where they had all met initially. He also booked a regular room in hopes of getting a brief tune-up from any of the ladies…preferably Tonjenae since he had yet to try her on fully.

"Thank you, ladies, for meeting me here today. I have a very unusual proposition for you, so I wanted us to meet in a more formal setting."

"I hope it's a job offer or something, 'cause we pretty much all lost our jobs messing around up here the other week," Tonjenae volunteered, then looked down at the floor. "My aunt is pissed because she counted on all of us to help with the bills."

Sherita nodded in agreement.

"Well, what I'm offering will improve all of your lives forever," Ron said, making the ladies excited. "I am willing to offer each of you ten thousand dollars to give birth to my child. I will pay five thousand when you get pregnant, and the other five thousand once you give birth and it is confirmed that the child is mine. Additionally, each of you will be able to move into my eleven-bedroom mansion, and your child will be made a beneficiary to my estate. Of course, while living with me, you'll want for nothing. You'll have everything at your disposal."

The girls were stunned by the indecent proposal. A few became extremely excited.

"Well, what about sex? Will we still be able to be with you sexually after the baby or no?" Shirleen asked.

"Anytime you want. However, there will be times when I might want to spend more time with one over another or take one of you on a trip to an exotic destination. I don't want to hear any drama. If you can't deal with the arrangement, then don't sign up for it. You can go on back to whatever life you had before."

"What about your wife? Will she be there, too?" Kennedy inquired.

"What are you worrying about her for? She's not our problem. It's his house, and if he says he wants us there, then that's that," Kendra told her sister.

"My wife will live in the house until she decides to move out, but she won't bother you in any way."

"So, are y'all getting a divorce, or do we gotta share you with her, as well?" Angela asked.

"I already let her know what was going to be. She wants no parts, so I guess she'll be leaving. With you carrying my child, legally, she can't bother any of you."

"Heyyy!" Kendra yelled, already implying that she was onboard with the proposal.

"This whole thing sounds crazy," Sherita said.

"Well, go find yourself another job and keep struggling," Sherrell told her. "To me, it beats getting pregnant by some bum-ass nigga that can't buy the baby diapers or milk."

"My niece or nephew will be my child's brother or sister," Sherita commented, shrugging her shoulders.

"Damn, bitch! You act like someone is forcing you to do something you don't want to do. Your problem is, you want

Mister Ron all to your fucking self," Erica snarled.

"Yeah, I do. Is that a problem?" Sherita spat back. "Would've had him to myself had I not let you come up to hang out with me for the weekend."

"Were you worried about having him to yourself when you laid down with him knowing he had a wife? No! So, stop acting so stupid," Tonjenae said.

The others agreed.

"You're free to go," Tonjenae added.

Ron stood, waiting to see what Sherita would do. She was clearly distressed by the proposal.

"Fine! Whatever! Momma's gonna be furious when she finds out," she said.

"We grown!" Toni reminded her. "Auntie Shirley would be furious if you came home with a baby that she had to take care of because you ain't got no job 'cause you busy fucking people's husbands, or you got knocked up by a man who can't do shit for you."

"Shoot, our momma would be pissed if we didn't jump on this offer. She wasn't even eighteen when Kendra was born, and she turned right around and got pregnant again by a different man 'cause she needed help buying diapers and formula. Nare one of our daddies bothered to hang around to see us born," Kennedy said. "Count me in."

"When do we get paid so I can stop working at that diner that only pays me three dollars an hour?" Sherrell asked.

"When you get pregnant," Erica reminded.

"Well, shoot, let's get busy then." Sherrell laughed.

"Damn, I'm on my period." Kendra pouted.

Angela raised her hand. "Same here."

"Aw hell, so am I," Toni said.

"I'm not!" Sherrell stated with excitement.

"So, is everyone in?" Ron asked.

The ladies looked around the conference table for validation from the others before all raising their hands, even

Sherita.

"I know everyone is anxious to get started, but today, I'm going to start with only two of you, and those two will be Tonjenae and Erica."

"YESSSS!" Erica cheered.

Tonjenae high-fived Erica.

"I'll send up lunch for the rest of you, and then I'll be in touch with you in the order that I want to see you."

"Today?" Sherrell asked.

"No, not today. Today, I only want the two I mentioned."

"Aww," she responded, trying to hide her disappointment.

"Ladies," he said, signaling for Erica and Tonjenae to go with him.

They were both excited and nervous.

Ron called for his car service to take them to a restaurant where they had lobster and champagne for lunch. He watched to see how both ladies adapted to their environment. Afterward, he stopped by his office to check on things. Then they returned to the hotel later that afternoon.

While at the hotel, Erica was confused because she only had to sit and watch as he devoted time to Tonjenae. Tonjenae's sexual skills pleased him. He could feel her intense passion for him, and he liked it. When he finished with her, he had his car service take Tonjenae back to Griffin, while he and Erica remained at the hotel until the next afternoon. When they left in his SUV, she didn't know where they were going, but she was glad he treated her like his number one.

12

Ava couldn't believe her eyes while watching the security monitor in her office and seeing some "child" getting out of Ron's truck and heading into their home, the two holding hands. She didn't know what to do. Ron had been quiet for the past two weeks and even had the nerve to continue sleeping in the same bed with her despite their declaration of war, although there was no intimacy. She assumed he was just being an asshole, thinking she'd go sleep in a different room. She refused to budge, though.

She watched the monitors while he gave the girl a grand tour of the home. However, when she noticed the pair go into Ron and Ava's master bedroom and close the door, she didn't know if she would have a heart attack, commit murder, or what. Not knowing what else to do in that moment, she called Eve on her phone. Unfortunately, none of her children were currently in the state. She hated involving their children in their marital woes, but this one was a crisis she had never dealt with.

"How long have they been in the room?" Eve asked.

"I don't know," Ava snapped. "Maybe about fifteen or twenty minutes now. If I go up there, I'm going to prison."

"Yeah, and we need you. Momma, I know this is very hard for you, but I promise we will pay his ass back. His ass is going down. Him and his bitch."

"I didn't tell you, but about two weeks ago, he told me that he was moving his new woman into the house, saying he loved her and she's having his baby. Then, he later added that there would be more than one woman."

"ARE YOU SERIOUS? Momma, why didn't you say

something before now?"

"I didn't think he was serious. Eventually, he ended up admitting he had just met the girl. Things have been quiet since then."

"So, he thinks he's just going to move bitches into your house? Did you remind him that the house is in your name, as well as most everything else?"

"No. I figured the less I reminded him of, the better, in case he's serious about waging this war with me."

"Okay, cool! His sick ass won't even see anything coming."

"That was my thought. Didn't think it would ever come to this, though."

"But what was he thinking, Momma?"

"I'd have to be insane to understand his logic. I figured he was insane when he transferred every one of his assets into my name a couple of years ago to prove to me that he was serious about never cheating again."

"How long are you going to let this shit go on? So now, he has basically booted you out of your own bedroom. You know Rashaun, Shara, and Jeremy will get locked up the minute they find out about this."

"That's why I don't want them to know anything just yet. I will give the fool enough rope to hang himself. If he wants to make babies with other women and whatever, then he'll be in for the rudest awakening yet. I figured it would be just a matter of time before a bastard baby popped up, which is why I planned for this day.

"You know, I never wanted to tarnish your father's image in your eyes, but unfortunately, he's decided to reveal himself to all of you."

"We all knew. That's why none of us can stand his ass. I just didn't want to see the obvious. I'm done trying to defend his ass. Are they still in the room?"

"Yes. I'm sure he wants me to walk in on them."

"Can you call the police to get them out? Don't you have friends there?"

"Even though his name is not on the house, he's still considered a tenant. So, it's not that simple. I don't want to show my hand until after everything is liquidated. By the time I'm done with his ass, he won't have money to afford a safety pin to put a cloth diaper on a baby. He'll be begging me for milk money."

"Please tell me you're not going to stay in that house, Momma. That shit will make you bat-shit crazy. It's making me crazy way over here. Go stay in one of our apartments until you get everything liquidated?"

"I still need to get all of my belongings out of the house. That's going to take at least two weeks."

"Momma, do you really want all that shit in that house that you shared with Daddy? No! Just take your personal items over to my apartment and stay out of that house. I should be back in town in a few days. And don't forget to add some cyanide to the pool so his bitches will burn the minute they get in it."

Ava laughed. "Ah, I see I taught you well, my child."

On the monitor, Ava noticed Ron exiting the bedroom and closing the door behind him.

"He just came out of the room alone in a bathrobe. Guess he must have worked up quite a thirst, because he went to the kitchen for the juice and two glasses."

"That's fucked up."

"Yeah, it is."

"Where's the girl?"

"I guess still in my bed."

"Damn! I'm going to need some Xanax behind this shit. I can't imagine how you're feeling."

"Yeah, a Xanax would be nice right about now. Especially since it looks like he's looking around for me."

"Wow! What a lowdown, dirty pig."

"Ava! You in here?" Ron called out as he got closer to her

office where she was sitting.

She quickly turned off her computer monitor along with the surveillance monitor and ran to hide when she saw him getting closer.

"Well, I'll be damned! She ain't even here," he mumbled as he walked out.

"What did he say?" Eve asked.

Ava wouldn't respond until she knew Ron was no longer within earshot.

"He's pissed because he thinks I'm not here," she whispered. "I hid behind the drape when I saw him coming."

"Why'd you hide?" Eve inquired.

"Why was he looking for me is the better question. Why was he mad that he couldn't find me in the house while he's draped in a fucking bathrobe, with a bitch in my bed, and while carrying around two glasses and a container of juice?"

"He wanted to rub it in."

"Exactly, and I wasn't going to let him have the satisfaction," Ava said, returning to her computer and turning on both monitors.

"Good! He is so evil. Before I thought he was just delusional, but that is pure evil. Momma, please go stay in my apartment tonight. Relax your nerves. I'm sure it's been rough sleeping in the same bed with him for the past week or so."

"Yes, it has."

"Then go."

"My stuff is in the bedroom."

"Don't take anything but your pocketbook. You can stop somewhere to buy toiletries and new clothes."

"Fine. He may have already seen my car when he came in."

"Take one of his other cars from the garage so he won't see you leaving. Plus, it'll piss on his last nerve. You know how he is about his stupid cars."

"True. Okay, I'll call you soon."

"Please do, Momma. Let me know when you get to my

apartment."

"Will do. Love you, my dear."

"I love you, too, Mom."

Ava collected as many files as she could, grabbed her pocketbook and keys, then slipped out of the house unnoticed.

*****

Out of spite, Ron kept Erica in his wife's bed all night, hoping she'd eventually return. He was beyond annoyed when the sun came up, but there was no interruption from Ava. He looked out of the window and saw her car still there, which baffled him.

Erica, on the other hand, was feeling every bit the queen that Ron had promised he'd make her feel. She knew he wanted his wife to see them together so she would know her new place. Erica, too, wanted his wife to see them together. She was in love with Ron but knew better than to behave territorially as Sherita did, which caused her to lose her position in Ron's life. Now, Ron treated Sherita like an afterthought, but she continued to hang around for whatever scraps of attention he threw her way. At that point, Erica loved Ron so much that she would have had his baby without looking for payment. She was hoping to be pregnant with his child already.

She spent close to three years in a sexual relationship with the bishop of her church, where she learned how to please a man. Aside from sex, he never made any effort to please her. Most of the time, he was more concerned with being pleased himself than trying to make sure she was sexually satisfied, as well. She longed to have all the fancy things the bishop's wife had and felt it was the lifestyle she wanted. Their consistent affair ended before her nineteenth birthday because she was getting too greedy for his time, and he didn't want to deal with her demands. Not long after, she tried having sex with a neighborhood boy, but then the boy let his friend come in to get some, as well, even though she didn't want to go along with it. They tagged her as a ho and sent her on her merry way after having their way with her. She heard they also had Kendra together, but Erica never mentioned it because she was still sticking to her lie that they were both lying on her, and she'd have to explain how she found out. She was so desperate for his sex that she begged her bishop to give her another chance. At first, he told her no because he heard she'd been sleeping around. However, he was gracious enough to allow her to keep practicing giving head on him. On occasion, she'd get him to give her what she desired, depending on how excited he became during the blowjobs.

Before the bishop, she was the longtime recipient of fingering from the other neighborhood pervert, the old man who owned one of the town's grocery stores. She had heard about his perverse reputation and was curious to find out on her own. That began when she was only thirteen-years-old. She enjoyed him so much that she'd go to the store often and hope no one would be around to prevent it. She first received oral sex from her mother's longtime boyfriend, who she seduced while her mother was at work. He felt he'd only be cheating on her mother if he were to penetrate Erica. By the time Bishop got to her, she was ready to have her cherry popped. It wasn't until she turned eighteen that her mother's boyfriend felt she was legal enough to have sex with, but then when her mother learned what was going on, she kicked her out of the house but stayed with the boyfriend, keeping a closer watch on him. Despite that, Erica maintained a close relationship with her mother, and her mother's boyfriend would try to sneak and see Erica any chance he could. Her strong sexual urges also had her going to visit the old man when she had no other options.

Being Ron's number one would mean she would no longer need the old store owner, the bishop, her mother's boyfriend, and none of the neighborhood boys. To share Ron with the others would be a small task to overcome since she was already used to sharing the sex partners in her life. Being brought into his wife's home, in their bed, without having to hide, felt like the ultimate prize. When Ron shared with Erica that he told his wife that he loved her, she felt like nothing could ever top that feeling.

13

"Hello," Ava whispered, answering the phone when Ron called.

"Hey, I was wondering where you are," he had the nerve to say.

Ava could hardly believe his gall but was humored by the fact that he didn't get the satisfaction he wanted.

"I'm just waking up. Is everything okay at the house?" she asked, trying not to laugh.

"Where are you? I was worried sick. I thought something might have happened to you."

"Oh no, I'm fine. Thanks for checking, though. Anyhow, I have to pee, so I'll chat later."

"But, where are you? Hello? Ava!"

He looked at the phone and saw she had hung up. He was furious. Wearing only a bathrobe, he went out to the garage to see which vehicle Ava had taken. Suddenly, his breathing shortened and his legs buckled from under him

"You bitch!" Ron yelled when he realized his red Ferrari 458 Italia Spider convertible was missing.

He attempted to call her back ten times in a row, but each time, the call went straight to voicemail. So, he texted her: *Why would you take my fucking Ferrari without my permission? You know I don't like anyone touching my cars. Especially that car.*

Activating the tracking device on his cell phone, it showed the Ferrari parked at his office address. He was confused because she told him that she had just awakened.

He ran inside his home office to view the video footage

from the company's office. He noticed Ava was in the building after midnight and had gone into his office. He wanted to kick himself for removing the video cameras from his office, because now he couldn't see what she was doing in there. He then tried to check the home security video to get an idea of when Ava left, but that was blank, too. Fear began setting in. The adage "a woman scorned" came to mind. He looked around the house for any clues of what she could be up to, but there were none.

At that moment, their maid, Guida, entered the house.

"Hey, good morning, Guida. Do you know where my wife might be? Did she tell you where she was going?"

"Good morning, Mr. Johnson. I spoke with your wife earlier. I'm a little surprised to see you here because she said she was vacationing in Miami, and I thought you might be with her," she responded, seeming confused. "I was off yesterday, remember?"

"Miami? What the fuck is my wife doing in Miami?"

"I'm sorry, but I don't want to get into any trouble," she said fearfully.

"Guida, you won't be in any trouble. What made you think I was with her? Did she tell you that?"

Guida's eyes widened, and she looked terrified. "I heard a man talking in the background."

"Oh, that was probably one of my sons," Ron said as he relaxed a bit and smiled.

Guida shook her head. "No, I doubt that very much."

"What the hell do you mean, you doubt it?"

"Please, Mr. Johnson. I want to mind my business. I don't want no trouble. Please."

Ron did a quick count to ten with his eyes closed and then exhaled.

"Guida, tell me what you know. NOW!" he yelled, startling her.

Tears formed in her eyes. "She said for him to stop playing

with her nipples while she's on the phone with me. She laughed a little and told him to stop. Then she said she'd call me back shortly because she had to deal with this nasty man."

Ron's fingers were clawed, and Guida quickly moved from out his reach when she saw the fire in his eyes. He looked around, found a vase, and shattered it into a million pieces when he threw it. Fearful, Guida sobbed hard.

Wearing one of Ron's robes, Erica came running down the stairs. "Baby, what's the matter?"

"Go get dressed. We have to go. I have some pressing matters to tend to," he ordered.

Erica ran upstairs with the quickness.

"Please, Mr. Johnson, I don't want to lose my job. I need this job. My grandsons are in college, and I can't let them down."

Ron calmed his temper some. "Don't worry; you won't lose your job."

"I will if Mrs. Johnson finds out I told you."

"I won't tell her on one condition," he said with a crooked, evil smile.

"Anything, please. I need this job."

"I want you to tell her that you saw me in our marital bed with a beautiful young lady. Tell her how soaking wet the sheets were when you changed the bedding, and tell her how happy I was when you saw us together," he instructed.

"You want me to lie to Mrs. Johnson?"

"That's not a lie," he yelled. "That beautiful young lady just spent the night with me, and we did make a mess on the sheets. So, that's not a lie," Ron responded, annoyed.

"But you said to tell her you were happy."

Still yelling, he said, "I am happy. I'm very happy. I just had the best night of my fucking life with a sexy woman, who will be moving here within the next few days I might add."

"Is Mrs. Johnson okay with that? She didn't mention anything to me about anyone moving in."

"I don't give a damn if that whore is alright with it or not. Then the bitch had the nerve to take my fucking Ferrari and leave it parked outside of my office building."

"She told you that?"

"No. I used my tracking device from my phone."

"Oh, okay. I hope the vandals didn't bother your car."

The center of Ron's forehead pulsated from the thought.

"God help the bitch if that happened. There will be no place on this earth for her to hide if that happens. Just make sure you tell her about my new lady. I wanted the bitch to see her for herself, but she never came home. Just like her ass to be spiteful."

"But, Mr. Johnson, why are you so angry that Mrs. Johnson is with someone if you're with someone? Are you planning to divorce Mrs. Johnson?"

"She's the one who wants a divorce, and she won't get one anytime soon. If she thinks her slick ass is going to try to get half of everything so she can spend it on whoever this new nigga is, she better think again. That's not happening. She can stay in this house, shut the fuck up, and watch me with my other women. Or she can kick rocks and leave with nothing. Let her kids take care of her since they were the ones who got her time and attention all these years. She didn't give a damn if I was happy or not. Well, now I am."

Erica returned dressed and ready to go. He summoned her over to him. Once she reached him, he took her into his arms and passionately kissed her for show.

"Yep, now I'm very happy. Erica, this is our housekeeper, Guida. Her parents are from Italy. She makes the best Italian food. She'll be looking out for you when you move in. She's typically here five days a week."

Still wrapped in Ron's arms, Erica beamed. "Nice to meet you, Miss Guida."

"Likewise," Guida replied with a half-smile. "I must get to work now. I have to get your room tidied and sweep up that broken glass.”

“Let me go throw some clothes on so I can go and get my car.”

“I’m hungry. Are we going to get some food?” Erica asked as Ron headed towards the stairs.

“Guida, please find some fruit and a muffin or something for my girl.”

“Yes, sir.”

When Guida took Erica into the kitchen, she asked, “You were together for a while?”

“No, not really. We just met like the other week. There were a bunch of us, but I guess he liked me the best.”

“Oh, interesting. Do you think it will be serious?”

“I feel like I love him. He told me that he loves me. That’s why he wanted me to come and see where I’d be living. He wants us to have a baby.”

Guida choked from the shock. “A baby?”

“Yes. He told us that he would pay each of us ten thousand dollars to have his baby. But, to be honest, I don’t even want the money. I just want to make him happy.”

“You said he’s going to pay us. How many are there?” Guida asked.

“There’s nine of us: me, Kendra, Kennedy, Toni, Tonjenae, Angela, Sherrell, Shirleen and Sherita. We all met him through Sherita, but once he and I met, he instantly fell in love with me. I knew we had special chemistry when we first met,” she bragged.

“But why the others? Why not just have a baby with only you?”

Erica’s smile faded, and she shrugged. “I think he said he wants to make sure our children inherit everything if he dies. Something about he doesn’t want his other children to get anything. He doesn’t want his wife to have anything either.”

“What if he does the same to you and your baby?” Guida asked.

"I doubt it. I'd do anything to please my man. I wouldn't put the kids' needs before his. That's what his wife did, and that's why he doesn't want her."

Hearing Ron approaching the kitchen, Guida decided to end her line of questioning. "Well, since you will be living here, I'll need you to write down your favorite foods so I can shop for them."

Erica lit up like a Christmas tree.

"Look at that beautiful smile, Guida," Ron said as he entered the kitchen. "Bet you never saw anything more beautiful."

"Yes, she is beautiful. Reminds me of my beautiful granddaughter." Guida smiled. "She'll be fifteen next week. I have to remember to buy her a gift."

Ron reached into his pocket and peeled off three one-hundred-dollar bills. "Here, get your granddaughter something nice."

"Oh, this is very generous of you, Mr. Johnson, but I can't take your money. Your wife already gave me five hundred dollars to get her a gift," Guida told him, refusing the money.

Annoyed and refusing to be outdone, Ron peeled off five more one-hundred-dollar bills. "Well, here's five hundred dollars to match her gift and an extra three hundred from me and Erica."

"This is too much. She's only a child."

"Add it to her college fund then. Anyhow, I have to get going. I called for a car service so I can go pick up my Ferrari. We have to go. Don't forget to tell my wife what I told you."

Ron took Erica's hand, and they were on their way.

Guida checked to make sure they were gone before going into Ava's office where she knew there was privacy. She hit a few buttons on her phone, then waited for the person on the other end to answer.

"Oh my God, Guida! You deserve an Oscar for that out-fucking-standing performance. You were brilliant," Ava screamed, laughing into the phone.

"Did the video come through well? I was afraid the camera moved when I jumped from him scaring the shit out of me."

"I got it all."

"Oh no! All the monitors just went off."

Just then, Ava appeared in her office. "Nah, I shut it off so it wouldn't catch me coming in."

Guida hugged Ava. "I'm so sorry you're going through this. Do know that I will do absolutely anything I can to help you burn his ass to the ground. That is just despicable. You know I got people back home to take care of matters such as these. Make people disappear just like that." She snapped her fingers.

Ava smiled. "I know, and I appreciate you so much. However, I just need for you to hang around on the inside a few more days while I try to get my stuff out of here. I plan to give him a dose of what he's been itching to have, as well."

"Not a problem. You know I'd do anything for you, but I'm not touching that nasty-ass bed. That's where I draw the line." She laughed while making the sign of a cross in front of her.

Ava cracked up. "Honey, I don't blame you. I should set that bitch on fire. Better yet, I'll take care of the bed. I have something for his bitch ass."

"Oh my goodness, I'm going to miss working for you. Just about twenty years. We had some wonderful times together. You never acted like a boss. Always a friend."

"Just think, your bank account will be bigger than your other boss' bank account once I'm finished with him." Ava laughed. "Girl, you had me cracking up when you lied and told him that I gave you five hundred dollars. Oh, and when you said the girl reminds you of your fifteen-year-old granddaughter, I lost it."

"'Cause I knew his overly competitive ass would try to outdo you. He's been like that since we were living back in Jersey. Not sure how you tolerated that. Guess I can say it now…arrogant prick!" She laughed. "And, yes, that girl looks about fifteen years old," Guida continued. "No disrespect, but child molester came to mind. Then she's dumb as a bag of rocks. Did you hear her talking about nine of them getting paid to have his babies?"

"Please! I'll bet my life that'll be an empty promise. By the time I'm done with his ass, he'll be borrowing bus fare from those hos. He thinks he's going to snatch my children's inheritance to hand off to some other random bitches he just met." Ava laughed heartily. "Anyhow, let me clean out my vault and get these files out of here. I'm sure that bitch was probably all up in my shit. If he asks you where my belongings are, tell him you cleared out the room for his company."

"Sure will. I'll help you load the car," Guida volunteered.

"I should set up a hidden video camera in the bedroom and let his dirty deeds be streamed live on social media from his account. Motherfucker wanna fuck with me? Did he really not know any better?" Ava laughed. "I need you to keep a watch out for him. Don't want the grimy bastard to catch me in here."

"Absolutely. Let's get to work."

"By the way, thanks for the ride."

14

"Hey, Dr. Morris. Thanks for seeing me on such short notice."

"It was a tight squeeze, but it's not often that I hear from you. Figured it must have been serious. How's your wife? She's usually with you. Well, except for when you're getting checked for an STD." Dr. Morris frowned. "Is that the reason for this visit?"

"Man, I don't know what the hell is going on. Look at this rash all over my body. They're turning into blisters."

Dr. Morris put on a pair of examination gloves and looked closely. "Yeah, that looks bad. I might have to admit you to the hospital and put you in isolation. This looks contagious."

"Am I going to die?" Ron panicked.

"First, we have to figure out what it is. Looks like a combination of a severe case of shingles and some form of contact dermatitis. Have you recently changed detergents or slept in unfamiliar beds?"

"No change in detergent as far as I know. I've been at a hotel a few times, but no one else has any problems. No rash. Nothing."

"When did this start? What about your wife? No rash on her? Shingles are very contagious, if that's what this is."

"As far as I know, my wife is fine. She ran off to Miami with another man. Bitch!"

Dr. Morris' eyes stretched behind his glasses, as if in shock. "Really?!"

"A few nights ago, I brought a young lady to stay with me at my house. She's perfectly fine. She has no rash or anything. I was at a hotel after that with one of my other ladies, but back in my bed by two o'clock that morning. I woke up itching. I took some Benadryl that next day and applied some cream, but it didn't help much. I even took several showers, but it didn't help relieve the itching. I ended up having to work from home that day. Yesterday, I had the housekeeper put on a fresh set of sheets, and now this morning, my body is covered with blisters. I mean, look at this shit. They're on my face, my neck, my back, my chest, my arms, my ass, my thighs, and my calves. The rash is everywhere, as well, even on my feet. I could hardly get dressed to come here. This is embarrassing. I don't want anyone to see me looking like this. I was going to go pick up my new lady today, but I don't even want her to see me looking this way or to catch anything if it is contagious."

"I'm sorry, but I'm going to have to admit you for a few days. If it is shingles, you are highly contagious. With you scratching and breaking the skin, other infections will eventually set in. I'd be concerned about your housekeeper's well-being, as well, since she cleans behind you. She'll need to get checked out, too."

"Doc, I can't stay in a hospital for a few days. My lady is waiting for me."

"You must not care too much about this lady if I'm telling you it might be contagious and you want to expose her. And I thought you were worried about her seeing you looking like this?" Dr. Morris pointed.

Ron shrugged, disgusted.

"I don't know if you're using protection or not," Dr. Morris continued, "but if the lady somehow becomes pregnant while you have an active case of shingles, it'll be passed on to the baby, and that won't be good. You'll pass on a lifetime of suffering for that child. Maybe even brain damage."

Ron sat on the exam table looking like he had seen a ghost.

"What's wrong?" Dr. Morris asked.

"We've been trying to get pregnant."

"Wow! So your marriage is over, I assume."

"That's how she wanted it. I wanted to work on my marriage, but she decided to skip off to Miami with some other motherfucker. What am I supposed to be doing in the meantime?"

"Ron, having an affair is one thing, but a baby? That's a big deal. You're not all that young, you know, and shingles tend to be lethal to people over fifty-five. You're almost sixty-two."

"Lethal? Lethal? Are you're trying to say I can die from this shit?!"

That's why we need to get you admitted as soon as possible. If you keep scratching like you're doing, that'll make it worse, and the last thing you want to do is OD on Benadryl. I can tell you're high right now."

"These things are itchy and painful. What am I supposed to do? I needed something."

"I understand. Now can I go ahead and get your admission set up? We'll have to dispose of these clothes, as well. No electronics in your room aside from the television provided for you."

"No electronics? Can I have my phone at least?"

"Nothing."

Ron was pissed. "Visitors?"

"Your immediate family can visit you. They'll have to wear a mask, gown, shoe covers, and gloves. Should I give your kids a call while I'm setting up your admission?"

"Yeah, call my daughter, Eve, and let her know her dad may be dying. She can call the others," Ron stated in a somber tone as a single tear fell from his eye.

"Let's not send everyone into a panic when we don't know for certain what's wrong with you. Now, what about your wife? Despite what is going on between the two of you, I'm sure she'd want to be here for you."

"You can let her know, but I don't want to see her ass."

Dr. Morris turned his head and rolled his eyes at Ron's

hypocrisy.

"Whatever you'd like. We need you to be completely comfortable. And stop rubbing your eyes. You don't want the shingles spreading to your eyes and causing you to go blind. Now, I'm going to get a room assigned for you. Be right back."

As soon as Dr. Morris left the room, Ron broke down and started sobbing. From the other side of the door, Dr. Morris could hear him placing a call and telling someone that he might be dying and didn't want her or the baby to catch whatever he had. Then he expressed that he loved her and would fight to get better so they could be happy together with their baby.

Dr. Morris stood by the door listening and fighting to keep from laughing.

*****

After being moved to an isolation room in the hospital, Ron asked Dr. Morris if he had spoken with Eve.

"Yes, I did. She said she'll be here as soon as she can. She said she has to find a flight because she's currently in California."

"Yes, my baby has her own successful import/export company and travels a lot. I was angry that she wouldn't work with me, so I never expressed to her how proud I am of her. Perhaps I'll tell her when she gets here."

Dr. Morris smiled. "You should. That would be nice. I also let her know to bring you some clothes for when you're discharged. When the virus gets under control, we should be able to get you a hospital phone to keep you from completely going crazy. Is the medicine starting to help with that itch?"

"Hell yeah! Got me sleepy."

"Oh, one more thing. You'll probably have to burn your mattress. I would hate for you to get re-infected. Maybe your family can arrange for hazardous waste management to get it out and get your bedroom sanitized before you get home.

Otherwise, you might end up right back in here."

"Ava's going to be pissed. She loved that bed. Paid like twenty thousand dollars for it. Man, she's gonna be mad. Well, let them know the bed has to go and whatever else."

Ron started falling asleep, and Dr. Morris took that as his cue to exit.

"You know y'all owe me big time for this, right?" Dr. Morris said, laughing as he got in the backseat of the car with Ava and his wife, who was a very close friend of Ava's.

15

"Good morning, Mr. Johnson. How are you feeling today?"

"I'm ready to get the hell out of this hospital. That's how I'm feeling," Ron snapped. "Who the hell are you, and where is Dr. Morris?"

"Unfortunately, Dr. Morris may have caught what you have and is in need of treatment, as well. Oh, and I'm Dr. Wozinski. Dr. Morris asked that I check in on you. We're really good friends," he answered, while standing at the foot of Ron's bed and looking at his chart.

"Dr. Morris is in this hospital, too? As a patient?"

"No, he chose to go to a facility in his hometown in North Carolina so he could be nearer to family…you know…just in case."

Ron covered his face. "Awww, man! I can't believe this shit is happening to me. I've been isolated in this room for six days and haven't had a single visitor. I wanted Dr. Morris to try reaching my family again, or at least grab my cell phone so he could call my lady for me. Do you think you could make a call from my cell for me?"

Dr. Wozinski held up both hands. "That would be an absolute negative, sir. First, we are prohibited from touching patient property. Besides, security locked up your phone. So, I have no access to it. Secondly, even if I could, I wouldn't since Dr. Morris has contracted what you have from making contact with you. Finally, I highly suggest you dispose of that phone to prevent getting infected again once you are discharged."

"Speaking of discharge, I'm hoping to be out of here by tomorrow. I've probably lost at least ten pounds in this place from the nasty food. Even worse, they forget to bring me a meal at least once a day."

"Oh wow! That's terrible. I'll speak with the nurses about that. As for when you'll be released, you'll be here for ten days. Especially with Dr. Morris now being sick. He also informed me that your housekeeper has taken ill. I think he said something about her missing her granddaughter's birthday."

"Oh, man! That is horrible. I can't believe it. Fine! I'll do the four extra days. Dr. Morris said he'd try to get me a hospital phone to use. You think I can get one now? I can call my office and have someone track down a way to reach my lady. I don't have her phone number memorized, but it's in my cell."

"Dr. Morris didn't mention anything about a phone, but I'll check into it. I'm not sure if phones are permitted in isolation."

"Also, can you find out where my daughter is? She was heading here several days ago, and no one's been able to reach her since. I'm worried sick that something may have happened to her."

"Mr. Johnson, if you lie here stressing, you'll only prolong your time here. Shingles will not heal if you're continually stressing. If you'd like, I can order something to help you relax your nerves. We really need you calm."

"It's hard to stay calm when I have people sticking me for blood ten times a day. I'm going to need a transfusion before I leave here."

"I understand. Everyone hates hospitals for the same reason. Between you and I, I hate them, as well. Cry like a baby when I have to get stuck." Dr. Wozinski laughed. "Well, I have rounds to make, so I'll check back tomorrow."

"Could you bring me some real food when you come back? I'm starving."

"I'll see what I can do. Take care."

Ron felt like he was going crazy in the hospital. There were times he considered sneaking out to at least make a phone call, but after hearing about Guida and Dr. Morris, he wasn't that selfish that he would risk getting anyone else sick. He became even more concerned about Erica. It was killing him that he had no way to check up on her to make sure she wasn't sick.

His television only had eight channels. Two of them were hospital and in-service related, talking mostly about different psychiatric conditions and trial medications. Another was PBS, and the other five had either volume or picture issues. His second evening in, he saw a beautiful nurse and tried to flirt with her. She was utterly disgusted, and he hadn't seen her since.

At least ten times per day, he wondered if Ava was behind everything happening to him, but then he'd dismiss it since she hadn't had the opportunity to see Erica with him. It was making him crazy trying to figure out who the guy could be that she ran off with and how long the affair had been going on. It also made him crazy how only the same gay, male nurse was available to give Ron sponge baths. He was not permitted to shower himself for reasons unknown to him. Additionally, the male nurse was the only one willing to rub Ron's medication on his entire body. That definitely made him think of his wife. Seemed like something spiteful she'd do. Ava could be nice, patient and tolerant, but if rubbed the wrong way, she showed a dark side. She had forgiven him for his indiscretions numerous times, and each time she'd forgive him, he would be afraid and slept with one eye open for some time afterwards, expecting some form of revenge. Nothing ever happened, though. Aside from the time when she gave their son a different name than the one they had planned without saying a word to him about it.

Ron was anxious to get back to his baby-making plans but didn't want to chance infecting the women or the babies, especially knowing Dr. Morris and Guida became ill. His mind wandered back to the fact that his children were missing and Eve never showed up. He wondered if news about Erica may have gotten to Eve from Guida, and that angered her and the others. He was determined he'd find a way to punish them all if they sided with his cheating wife. The thought made him want to rip out the two IVs he had in each arm and leave.

Everything seemed to be making him crazy in there. If he didn't know any better, he would blame it on whatever they were injecting into his IVs. The clock on the wall was even playing tricks on him. It seemed as if it was moving super slow.

Speaking of time, like clockwork, the flamboyant, gay nurse came busting through the set of doors to the room and announced, "Bath time!"

16

"Momma went straight gangster on Pops. This will always serve as a reminder to never cross a woman," Rashaun said, as he laughed while looking around the house, which was emptied with the exception of some of Ron's clothes that they placed in one of his cars in the garage.

"His bitch behind had it coming long, long, long ago," Shara added.

"I'm still trying to figure out how she managed to have him locked up on an involuntary psych hold," Rashaun said, laughing hysterically to the point of tears.

Eve laughed, as well. "He thinks he's in the infectious disease isolation unit."

They all laughed at that.

"Like I said, straight gangster," said Rashaun.

"I know we're here laughing and all, but what if Daddy would have really died? I wouldn't be able to live with myself." Ariana pouted.

"And what if our mother suffered a heart attack, stroke, or a panic attack…or even contracted AIDS as a result of all his adulterous acts? How would you have felt about that shit? He had the nerve to bring that bitch into her house and slept with the ho in Momma's bed?" Eve said, getting worked up. "Every time I think about hearing my mother in distress that afternoon… Nah, he can drop fucking dead." Tears formed in her eyes.

Jeremy hugged Eve. "Don't worry, sis, Mom will be good from here on out, and Pops will get what the fuck he deserves."

"I know one thing, I wish Mom and Guida could have

really found some shingles virus to put in that bed. Him and his bitches would have been all fucked up," Eve added.

"She didn't want to chance him dying and her catching a murder case, but hell, that poison ivy worked. Got his grimy ass sitting up in that hospital going mad, thinking he's got the shingles," Shara said.

Everyone erupted in laughter.

"I just wish they had put him in a room with other crazy patients to really fuck with him," Shara continued. "Now THAT would have been perfect."

The others nodded in agreement.

"I'm going to kind of miss this house. I was just starting to get used to it," Rashaun said.

"Why? We didn't grow up in this house and never even got to live in it. We only had that five-bedroom house when we first moved to Georgia," Ariana reminded her younger brother. "He talked Momma into getting this house for the so-called grandkids. He was probably plotting the whole time to have a bunch of bitches living in here."

"Well, he was definitely a jackass to put the house in Momma's name." Shara said.

"Didn't he claim it was her Mother's Day gift or something?" Jeremy asked.

"He couldn't put his name on it while he still had the other house in his name or something like that. They never got around to adding him on the deed for this house. Momma said she has to give him a formal eviction. She said she wants to wait until he moves all those girls in the house," Eve shared with the others.

Everyone laughed again.

"I'm glad Momma's in Miami now catching her tan," Ariana said, laughing. "And took Guida with her."

"Dr. Morris' wife, Mrs. Gail, went with them, too, while Dr. Morris went golfing with his boys," Eve corrected.

"I was surprised Dr. Morris went along with everything," Ariana said.

"Money talks." Shara winked. "But, on the real tip, Dr. Morris can easily say, in his professional opinion, your father was going crazy and was in desperate need of being locked up. He is a threat to himself and society."

"True," Ariana nodded.

"Okay, y'all. You ready to head over to the hospital to visit that wretched old man?" Jeremy asked. "Everybody got their game faces ready?"

"I don't know how I'm going to keep from laughing," Ariana said.

"Well, maybe we should all laugh at his ass and tell him he deserves it since Guida told us about his other woman he brought to the house," Shara volunteered.

"No! We gotta stick with the game plan. When he gets his phone back with the virus I put in it, I don't want him to think we did something," Jeremy said, holding up Ron's phone. "The minute he tries to make a call or hit the send button on his text, the phone will die."

Rashaun lifted his hand for a fist bump with Jeremy.

"Damn, you the man! I'm so proud of my big brother. All of y'all, for real. I know we be fighting and acting stupid all the time because y'all can't accept the fact that I'm Momma's favorite, but…"

The others started roughing him up as they playfully disagreed.

"Shara, you got that extra poison ivy powder to sprinkle in his bed?" Eve asked.

"Sure do," Shara said, holding up the small plastic bag.

"Then, I guess we're ready to go now," Eve said, heading to the door.

"Poor Daddy! Poor, poor Daddy," Rashaun sadly said while walking to the door. "Hey, I'm getting my practice in. You know it's going to take some work to sound convincing. I'm sure Ariana got this on lock since she's an actress."

"And you know this, man!" Ariana said in her Chris Tucker impersonation, then laughed.

17

A stern, no-nonsense security officer returned all of Ron's personal items the day of his discharge. As dumb luck would have it, Ron's phone died the second he got it back and tried to call Erica. Unable to retrieve any information from his phone, he felt the need to make a pit stop by his office to try to locate Sherita's number from her personnel file so he could track down Erica.

He stayed in the hospital for a total of fifteen days. When his kids told him about their mother still in Miami with some guy, it made him start itching again and more blisters formed. It seemed to him that they were not her ally since she was seeing some other man, and that made Ron somewhat glad. They seemed very upset. Ron suggested Rashaun go to Miami to punch the guy out, but suddenly, his son seemed to have a conscience about going around hitting adults. He was furious when the kids said they had hazmat come to collect not only the mattress, but also the bedroom furniture because they didn't want him to get sick again. They told him about how bad they felt for Guida and that her family from Jersey had to take her back there because she wasn't doing well. He told them about Dr. Morris also being sick, and they seemed shocked by the news.

Now at the office, Ron searched for Sherita's personnel file but couldn't find it. He had never been to their homes, so he was unsure where to go to find them. Out of desperation, he drove all the way to Griffin. He hadn't even gone home yet, even though he was advised to get plenty of bedrest. Thankfully, they lived in a small neighborhood, so he was sure he would be able to find at least one of the ladies.

"Excuse me, would you be able to tell me where I might find Erica…Erica Dinkins," Ron asked a tall, plump, elderly gentleman who was getting in his Mercedes-Benz.

"Sure do. I'm the bishop at her church. Is there a problem?"

"No. No problem. I'm a friend from Atlanta. My phone died, and I lost all my contacts. I wanted to talk to her about some work. I know she's been looking for work," he lied to the bishop, who looked at him suspiciously.

His face lit up. "Oh, that's wonderful. I'm sure that would make her very happy. I just saw her last night at the church. She was a little upset because she said she's having some financial issues. She has a close friend, Toni. They usually hang together a lot. Toni has a cousin named Sherrell who works up the street at the diner. I'm not sure when she works, but Sherrell might be able to tell you where they are. They used to work in that store over there a few weeks back. I think she said they lost their jobs because they went to Atlanta with Sherrell's elder sister, Sherita."

"Thank you so much. I appreciate the information."

Actually, Ron was annoyed that the bishop felt comfortable sharing so much information with someone who was nothing more than a stranger to him. Originally from New York and New Jersey, Ron wasn't used to telling people's business or having it told to him. However, he noticed that was a common trait in Georgia.

Ron found the diner, but Sherrell was not there. So, he continued riding around until he finally spotted Kendra swatting away some young boys who were trying to touch on her curvaceous bottom. Ron honked his horn, and Kendra came running.

"Oh my goodness! I'm so happy to see you. I heard you were in the hospital, but then no one never heard anything else."

"I got out a couple of hours ago. They kept me in isolation for fifteen days. I couldn't have a phone or any other type of electronics in the room. I just got my phone back today. It powered on just fine, but when I went to make a call, it died."

"Damn! That's messed up. Are you okay now?"

"I guess. I'm sure they wouldn't have let me out if I wasn't. Why are you still standing out there? Get in."

Kendra jumped into the passenger seat, and Ron pulled off away from the eyes of those who were watching nearby.

"Where are the others?" Ron inquired.

"I don't really be keeping up with them. I be making myself a few dollars braiding hair. I told my momma about your plan, and she was excited. Then we didn't hear from you, so we didn't know what to think. Does the offer still stand?"

"Absolutely. That's why I came here before I even went home."

Kendra was extremely happy. "I wanna kiss you when I can. Is that alright?"

Ron pulled over and gave Kendra a kiss that let her know that he was very happy to see her.

"I missed you. Felt like I've been locked away for at least a year."

That made Kendra smile. "I missed you, too. Can we go somewhere today, or are you still sick?"

"I'm ready to take you and Erica home with me tonight."

"I heard you took Erica to your house. She said it was super big and you got a housekeeper, too."

"Yeah, well, I had one. She also became ill. That's why I've been worried sick about Erica. They had to remove the bed from my home to make sure I didn't get sick again."

"Damn! That's crazy. She's doing fine. I know where she lives. We can ride by there."

Truthfully, Kendra didn't want to find Erica. She wanted Ron all to herself, but she knew he wouldn't stop turning over stones looking for Erica until he found her. She didn't want to lie to him by saying she didn't know where Erica lived, because she knew there'd be hell to pay once he found out she lied.

"Great!"

They rode by Erica's place. Ron was shocked by what he saw. Her home looked like a shoebox in Ron's closet.

"She lives here with her family?" Ron asked Kendra.

"Nah, Erica got her own place. Her momma don't want any grown woman around her cheating man, so Erica had to go."

"Wow! She didn't tell me that. I thought she had a great relationship with her mother. That's how she made it sound," Ron said.

"Oh, don't get it twisted. Erica and her momma are thick as thieves. They're real cool. It's just she doesn't want her man to be looking at her daughter."

"That's sad. Anyhow, can you go and get her?"

"Sure." Kendra got out of the car, and while Ron watched, she tugged at her shorts that were riding up into her ample bottom.

Not even a minute after Kendra knocked on the door, Erica came out, obviously crying. That crushed Ron. He got out of the car, and she ran into his arms, holding him for dear life.

"Get what you need out of there. It's time for you to come home where you belong," he told her.

Since he didn't know what to expect at his house, he decided to bring only the two ladies, figured they could return the next day for their cars and other belongings. He decided the others could come the day after.

When they were on the highway, Erica blurted from the back seat, "I'm pregnant."

Ron was stunned, and Kendra seemed annoyed since she had yet to become pregnant.

"Oh wow! That's wonderful news. Are you sure?" he asked.

"I did a test, and it was positive. I even went to the clinic for a test. It was positive, too. I was so scared. I didn't know what to do. I didn't know if you were coming back or what."

"I told you I'd be back for you. I didn't think they would keep me in the hospital for so long. Then I didn't have access to my phone. I came to get you before even going home."

Erica had the widest smile. Kendra, on the other hand, was already bothered by Ron's blatant favoritism of Erica and the news that Erica was already pregnant. She regretted showing Ron where Erica lived.

"Well, I guess you and I are going to have to put in overtime to get this baby made," Kendra told Ron, hoping to get under Erica's skin.

"Yes, I guess we will," Ron agreed, then redirected his attention back to Erica. "I ran into your bishop, and he told me that you went to see him last night because you were in a financial bind. I apologize. I really didn't expect to be gone so long."

Kendra picked up on Erica's panicked look. She was all too familiar with what "seeing the bishop" meant. She'd been seeing the bishop for years herself. Kendra had a pregnancy scare a couple of months back, and the bishop told her that she needed to get on some kind of birth control. However, despite the lack of birth control, they had sex a few days ago, and he fed her a morning after pill as a precaution. As much as she enjoyed sex with the bishop, she had nothing to gain from being with him. At times, an entire month or two would go by, and he wouldn't touch her, causing her to feel rejected. That typically meant he was busy with someone else. Unlike Ron's wife, the bishop's wife didn't care what he did since she was living very well. There were even times she would call Kendra to let her know the bishop wanted to see her. The first lady was a very attractive, 37-year-old woman who was married to the 66-year-old bishop. They shared four children. He had two older children from his first wife, who died about a month before he remarried.

Kendra didn't know the extent of Bishop's sexual relationship with Erica, but she knew that going to see the bishop for money at night meant you were going to give up something. Kendra couldn't help but wonder if the baby Erica was carrying belonged to Ron or the bishop, and she planned on using that bit of information against Erica every chance she could. Furthermore, she wasn't too fond of Erica because Ron seemed to be most concerned with Erica's happiness than anyone else's.

Yeah, she planned on having a chat with Erica, and if that didn't go well, then she'd have a chat with Ron. Maybe she could get Erica booted out of the number one spot and claim it for herself.

18

Ron wanted to cry from anger when he walked into his house and found it bare. The furniture, electronics, dishes, appliances, ceiling fixtures, window treatments, the Calacatta marble counter top, luxury toilets, the Italian white Carrara marble floor tile in the foyer and master bathroom, and every expensive piece of molding were gone. Even the plumbing fixtures…GONE!

He was about to use his phone to call the police, but then remembered he had yet to replace his phone. So, he used Erica's phone to report that his wife cleaned out the entire house. He was instructed to take the matter up in divorce court.

He had the ladies get into his Mercedes-Benz SUV and was further disturbed when he saw his gas tank was nearly empty. He didn't see any extra mileage, but he was pretty certain his tank had been just about full when he last parked it. He drove to a nearby hotel and attempted to get a suite.

"I'm sorry, sir, but would you happen to have another credit card?" the desk agent asked. "This one doesn't seem to be working,"

Ron pulled out his black American Express card and handed it to her. "I don't know why that wouldn't work. I have at least a ten-thousand-dollar credit line on that card."

"I don't know why, but this one also is showing declined. It's actually saying for me to confiscate the card."

"Are you fucking serious? What the hell is going on?" he shouted.

"Sir, you're going to have to lower your voice and leave quietly before I call security to escort you out."

Ron covered his face. He couldn't believe what was happening. "I do apologize. Could you please try another card for me?"

"No, sir. You're going to have to leave immediately."

"Bitch! You and my wife…BITCHES!" Ron shouted as he went to collect Erica and Kendra, who were seated in the reception area.

The agent signaled for security. Ron held up his hands, letting them know he was leaving.

"What happened?" Erica asked when they were back in his truck.

"Just shut the fuck up. I can't think. That bitch did this shit. I know she did. She wants a war; I'll give her a fucking war. She fucked with the wrong motherfucker!"

Erica was startled to tears, while Kendra found herself smirking at Erica's discomfort.

The gas light came on, and Ron stopped for gas. Again, his credit cards and bank cards were all declined. That infuriated him even more. He ended up going inside to pay with cash. Next, he stopped at a cell phone store to get a new phone. For a reason unknown to the sales clerk, they were unable to offer him a new phone on credit and suggested he use his insurance to have his phone repaired. Ron didn't have enough cash to buy a phone at the full price, and the banks were already closed. So, he had no choice but to head back to his office to grab a couple of company credit cards along with some cash. Before leaving, he called to make sure the cards were valid. Happy to have something, he took off and found a hotel for the trio.

The ladies did what they could to get Ron to relax. One minute, he would be calm, and the next, he would be threatening to kill Ava. It made him feel better when the two ladies would also call Ava a bitch and encourage him to pay her back.

While at the hotel, he decided to call American Express to figure out what had happened with his personal card. When they asked for his driver's license number to verify his identity, that is when he realized his license was missing. He was positive he had it when he went to the hospital and when he checked out. Then he figured he must have left it downstairs when he checked into the hotel. So, he put his clothes back on to go down to get it, but the front desk agent who checked him in had already left, and the agent for the next shift didn't see it anywhere.

He called American Express again to let them know he lost his license, but they refused to help him. He was so upset that he didn't even want sex.

He paced the floor most of the night and was out the door at the onset of business hours, leaving the ladies sleeping.

His first stop was the bank.

"I'm not really supposed to help you without your ID, but since I've seen you around, I might be able to help," the young lady told him.

"I appreciate this, and I'll definitely make it up to you," he said, shifting into flirt mode despite the wedding ring she wore.

"I see the one card was maxed out a few weeks ago at a hotel…Marriott. Also, a steak restaurant. The steak restaurant charge alone is close to seven thousand dollars. The hotel charge is over four thousand. Actually, you've overdrawn this card. Oh, wait, I see your cards were all reported stolen a couple of weeks ago…almost three weeks now. Are you saying you didn't report them stolen? There hasn't been any attempted activity on them since."

"Absolutely not! I've been in the hospital for fifteen days and just got out yesterday."

"Hmm, interesting, but the report was made by you sixteen…seventeen days ago. That would have been before you went to the hospital. I see a Ferrari kit was ordered on one of the cards the same day before the report."

"Someone is setting me up!" Ron yelled in a whisper.

"So you didn't order something from Ferrari totaling almost two thousand dollars?" the woman asked suspiciously.

"Well, yeah, I did place that order because my crazy wife

left my car parked out in the elements."

"Well, whoever verified your account information was able to sufficiently provide your identity."

"It was probably one of my sons. I don't know, but it wasn't me. Now, could you use funds from my bank account to clear the credit card debt so I can use my cards again?"

"I'm sorry, but one, the cards are already reported as stolen, which means there's no way to reactivate them. Two, your accounts are currently under investigation, and three, we've tried to get the funds from your bank account, but there weren't enough to cover your overdraft."

"Are you fucking serious? This is a joke, right?"

"Mr. Johnson, I am a good Christian woman who has been trying to help you. Please watch your language with me. Like I said before, I'm not even supposed to be helping you without ID, and no, this is not a joke. I see you made a five-thousand-dollar cash withdrawal the same day as the charge from the steak restaurant. You do stuff like that and it's bound to draw attention. That withdrawal was here in this branch."

"We have over a million in this bank alone. What do you mean there weren't enough funds?"

"Looking over your account, I don't see a million dollars, but I do see many cash withdrawals in the amount of five thousand dollars almost weekly. I don't see any recent deposits other than interest. It's very common for people to spend like that and later can't account.

"How much is in my wife's account? Did she pull money from my accounts to put into hers?"

"I'm sorry, I can't discuss your wife's accounts without her permission."

"What about our joint accounts? How much is in there?" Ron asked, sounding like a drug fiend.

The banker looked surprised. "Sir, that account was closed almost seven years ago."

"Seven years ago? What the fuck do you mean, seven years ago? Where's my money from that account then?"

"Sir, I'm going to have to ask you to leave now. That's the second time you've disrespected me like that. I've asked you to refrain from using profanity, and I'm done helping you."

"Fuck you, you ugly bitch! You're just mad I don't want you."

"If you don't leave right now, I will press this button and have you locked up. Leave! Now!" she ordered with her hand under her desk.

Ron made a quick exit. He tried three other banks, but no one would help him without ID. He went by the DMV to get a new license but was unable to because he needed other ID. He had no idea where any of his papers were since Ava always handled everything. His next stop was to purchase a new phone and then go to Home Depot to purchase new fixtures and appliances so he could move back into his home with his women. He went to the bed store to order ten new beds. Nothing as expensive as the one he had with his wife, though. He charged all of his purchases to his unlimited company credit card and used the ATMs to get some extra cash.

When he returned to the hotel and found the two ladies looking depressed, he had them get dressed for a night out on the town. That lifted their spirits.

The past couple of weeks had been rough for him. Still, he was determined to shake it off at least for the night.

If things couldn't get any worse, he zipped past a police car that he didn't see and ran a red light while rubbing his hand between Kendra's thick thighs. The shots of Courvoisier he chugged before leaving the hotel and the fact he didn't have his driver's license didn't play in his favor.

When the officer let Ron know he'd have to place him under arrest, he began putting up a fight. Erica begged him to stop resisting when she saw the officer place his hand on his gun. The ladies became even more frantic when three more police cars quickly pulled up. While Ron lay handcuffed on the ground, one officer informed the others that Ron had just been released from a 51-50 the day before.

"Oh, you must not have spent enough time in the looney bin, huh?" one cop said, laughing.

A commanding officer on the scene instructed the arresting officer to take him back to the hospital.

"Hospital? Looney bin? What are you talking about? I had shingles and was hospitalized. I'm not crazy!" Ron yelled.

Hospital or jail? Your choice," the commanding officer asked.

"Oh my God! My wife! I know she's behind this."

"Your wife made you run a red light in front of a police officer, with alcohol on your breath and no driver's license?" he asked Ron.

Ron had no explanation for that.

"Erica, take my truck and drive back to the hotel. Find out where they're taking me and send a lawyer," Ron instructed.

"Erica, is it?"

"Yes," she responded to the commanding officer.

"Do you have a valid driver's license?"

"Yes, sir." She smiled.

"Now, Erica, I need you to be honest with me: You appear to be a minor. Have you been drinking alcohol tonight with your boyfriend here? 'Cause if you were, I don't think you want to get behind that wheel tonight. Also, if I have to look at your license and find that you are indeed a minor, particularly one who has been consuming alcohol, that won't work out very well for you."

"Oh my God! This is insane. What's supposed to happen to my truck?" Ron asked before Erica could speak up.

"Sir," one of the officers said to the commanding officer, "we just found a large amount of cash in the car. There's at least three thousand dollars here in an envelope."

"Interesting," the commanding officer said. "Care to explain?" he asked Ron.

"I'm a very successful businessman. I own Johnson Incorporated, and I was taking these ladies to dinner. I picked up some cash earlier to take them."

"Three thousand dollars for a dinner? Must be some dinner you were planning."

"If you look in my wallet, you'll see several credit cards, even a black American Express, as well as a couple of company credit cards. All have my name on them."

"See, the problem with all of that is, we have no way of proving who you are because you don't have a picture ID."

"AVA, I HATE YOU!" Ron yelled out in frustration.

"Ava? Ava Johnson? Is that your wife?" the commanding officer asked.

"Yes, and I think she's out to get me." Ron broke down sobbing while still lying face down on the ground in handcuffs.

The arresting officer told the commanding officer, "Well, at least now the 51-50 makes sense."

The officers all laughed, while Ron had no idea what that meant.

"Mr. Johnson, today is your lucky day. Ava is a very close friend of my wife and my mother. They'd be really pissed if they found out I caused your wife any grief. So, here's what we're going to do. You're going to take a taxi back home, and tomorrow, when you are sober, you can go to the tow yard and pick up your truck with some valid identification. And I highly suggest you lose the bimbos before that angers my wife, as well.

Ron wanted to argue but decided to just agree and say thank you. He watched as his $140,000 truck was towed away. He had no idea how he'd be able to get another ID without Ava's help, which he knew she'd never do.

They took a taxi back to the hotel and was forced to eat dinner there, which had him wondering why he didn't do that in the first place. After dinner, they returned to the room for a night of sinfully, unadulterated sex.

19

"Damn, I love that man!" Erica said while rolling on the bed like a person in love. "I can't wait for our baby to be born."

"*If* it's his baby," Kendra responded with disdain.

Erica laughed. "Girl, don't be hating on me because I got pregnant first and because Ron prefers being with me instead of you. Doesn't even matter that you give him your butthole. The man wants who he wants."

Kendra stuck up her middle finger at Erica.

"Come to think of it," Erica continued. "I don't understand where all this shade is coming from when I have to share his ass with you and seven others."

"Is that really Ron's baby or do you even know who the father is?"

"What the hell are you talking about? Yes, Ron is the father. Why would I lie about something like that?"

"For the money. For the status. To get up out of that box you live in. That's why you would lie, and then hope when he finds out the truth nine months from now, he'll be too in love with you to let go."

"He's already very much in love with me. He came to Griffin looking for me when he got out of the hospital, not you. He just ran into you first and used you to find me. You wouldn't even be here right now, just like the others, had he saw me first. So, I think that says it all. When he was being admitted into the hospital, who did he call? Me! Not anyone else. Not even his kids. Now, I'd highly suggest you treat me a little kinder before I let Ron know you're in here hating on me and giving me a hard way to go, hoping I lose his baby. I don't think he would like that at all, and he might just send your ass back to Griffin empty handed."

"I want you to tell him. I really do," Kendra dared. "'Cause when you do, I can give him the entire backstory on Bishop Rogers…the one you just went to see for some money the other night while supposedly carrying Ron's baby."

Erica's eyes widened and her mouth dropped open as she quickly sat up.

"Yeah, bitch, I know all about that. I know you be messing with old man Fredrick in the backroom of his little rundown store *and* your momma's boyfriend, who I saw coming out of your house in the middle of the night just last week, while the man you so-call love was in the hospital. I also know about them boys you let run a train on your ass a few months ago. Now, close your mouth, bitch, 'cause ain't much that gets by Kendra in that little ass town."

"I don't know what you're talking about," Erica said, feeling a sudden need to cover up her nudity.

"Like hell you don't know. But, nonetheless, I'll tell Ron all about Bishop and let him decide for himself since he does know you went to see him just the other night."

"Why would you do that and upset him like that? He's been having a really rough time, and you'd do that shit to him?"

"I sho'nuf will and then stick a titty in his mouth to make him feel better when you're gone."

"So why are you bringing all this up now? What do you want?"

"I really don't want you here, but since you are, I want you to step out of the spotlight before I see to it that you get booted out of the spotlight."

"Are you fucking serious? I can't control how he feels about me. If I get quiet, he'll know something is up, and that'll only make him pay more attention to me."

"Which would you rather happen? You can make yourself less noticeable, or I can draw attention to the fact that you've been drinking plenty of alcohol while being so-called pregnant.

Then I'll point out that the reason you might be doing all that drinking is because you ain't sure who the daddy is," Kendra dared. "Or maybe because you're not really pregnant. Just hoping to hurry up and get pregnant."

Tears formed in Erica's eyes. The last thing she wanted was for Ron to find out about her escapades with her mother's boyfriend, who would come to check up on her every now and again, and the sex she indeed had with the bishop just a couple of nights ago.

"I really am pregnant, and I'm not trying to lose my baby. I'm just stressed out with everything going on. He told me he was going to be in the hospital for just a couple of days, and might be dying, but then I don't hear anything from him. Anyone would be worried, especially when they're pregnant. We have to stay stuck in a hotel room, and we don't know for how long or what's happening. He was about to go to jail last night…or worse, get shot. Maybe even us. It seems like his wife is doing crazy things to him, probably 'cause she's mad he don't want her no more. Is she going to come after me, too? I'm the one who was in his wife's house having sex with him in her bed. That's why I'm stressed out and was drinking last night."

Kendra lightened up on Erica. "Yeah, this shit is really stressing me out, too. I've been worried about us getting pregnant and then him not being able to pay us or take care of us because of his bitter wife taking everything in the divorce. We need that money."

"Exactly! Can you imagine me having this baby and then having to raise it in that little place I got in Griffin? That would be fucked up. That's why I'm trying to do anything to keep him happy. I can't go back there."

Kendra softened up as she thought about that scenario.

"Okay, just stop being a bitch to me, or else I'ma tell it all."

"I promise. Oh, and for the record, he had his hand all up in *your* coochie when we got pulled over last night. So, it's not like he be all over me all the time." Erica laughed. "Y'all was so deep into that shit that neither of you saw the light change or the policeman sitting there just watching."

"What were you doing in the backseat? You didn't see the light or the police?"

"Hell no! I was making myself feel good. I was trying to feel what you were feeling."

"Damn, that shit was feeling good, too." Kendra laughed. "Did you hear when that racist motherfucker had the nerve to call us bimbos?"

"I was so stressed, I didn't even hear him. Shit, I thought I was about to go to jail for underage drinking. I thought they were going to check my driver's license."

"Yeah, that shit was scary."

A knock at the door interrupted them.

"Damn, we didn't order breakfast yet. It's getting late. I wonder who that is knocking."

20

Ron knew his day would be a difficult one. He had to somehow find a way to get his home safe combination so he could retrieve his passport and take it to the DMV for a new driver's license. Then there was the business of picking up his truck from the tow yard.

"Hey, Ariana sweetie," he said, calling her from his office phone.

"Daddy?" she asked as if suddenly uncertain of her father's voice.

"Yes, sweetie." He tried to be as nice as possible despite being disturbed about not hearing from any of them except for their one hospital visit and the possibility that they helped their mother empty out his home.

"Oh, hey. What's up? I'm kind of busy right now. I'm working on a commercial."

"Wow! Really? That's wonderful! What kind of commercial?"

"Daddy, I can't talk right now. What did you want?" she asked, sharply shutting him down from having small talk.

"I need the safe combination for my bedroom safe, and I can't find it. I thought it was in my sock drawer, but–"

"I don't know where it is. You're gonna have to ask Momma, but I have to go now. Bye!" she quickly said and ended the call.

Calling Ava was the last thing he wanted to do, and he was pretty certain Ariana already knew that much when she made the suggestion. Instead, he tried Eve.

"Hey, sweetie, this is Daddy."

Eve hesitated before speaking. "Oh…hey…what's up?"

"Did I wake you? You sound like you were sleeping?"

"I'm in Phoenix. I *was* sleeping," she snapped.

"Oh, I'm so sorry, dear. I was trying to find the combination to my safe so I can get my papers out. It was in my sock drawer, but since everything is gone, I'm not sure where it could be."

"I don't know. Check inside the suitcase in your Lexus. I think that's where I put that stuff from your sock drawer. I had to get that stuff out quickly for the hazmat people to come in and fumigate the house."

Ron was seething inside because he knew she was full of shit, but he didn't want to upset her just in case he had to call her back after checking.

"If it's not there, call Mom," she continued. "She has all that information somewhere, I'm sure."

"Well, I'm trying not to have to call her if I don't have to."

"Look, I don't mean to be rude, but I'm exhausted. I just hit the pillow like two hours ago, and I have a long day ahead of me. Call me later if you can't find it."

She didn't give him much opportunity to say anything else before she hung up. His next dilemma was to figure out where were the keys to his Lexus. There used to be a rack in the kitchen that held most of the car keys, but that, too, was gone.

Nonetheless, he made his journey to his home, found the Lexus keys in the garage, located the suitcase with the combination inside, and was able to access his safe. But, before making it back inside to the safe, he looked in each car, wondering where his massive number of suits were stored as well as his extensive dress shoe collection. Chalking it up to some more of Ava's doing, he went on to check his safe. There he found his passport, birth certificate, social security card, an insurance policy, and over twenty thousand dollars in cash. He was beyond excited. He thought there was much more than that, but then he knew he'd been known to pinch off of it quite often.

His first stop was to the DMV to get his license. By the time he left there to go to the tow yard by way of a taxi, the front office was already closed. That meant he wouldn't be able to pick up his truck until the following day. The bank was also closed; again, he would have to wait until the following day to take care of that business. Excited to have a little bit of normalcy back in his life, he called for Tonjenae and Angela to meet them at the hotel, where he had reserved another room. He was ready to accomplish his mission. Particularly after being lied to and blown off by his daughters.

When he entered the hotel room, Erica happily greeted him.

"Hey, baby. Did you get my message? I hadn't heard back from you."

"No. What message? I've been meaning to check up on you and also let you know Tonjenae and Angela are on their way up. A lot of the stuff will be delivered tomorrow to the house. I should be able to run and pick up my truck tomorrow, as well. I didn't make it there in time today because I was stuck at the DMV all day trying to get a new license."

"That's what we were trying to reach you about," Kendra said. "A lady brought your license up this morning after you left. We texted you a few times, but you didn't answer. We didn't call because we didn't want to make you angry."

"Are you fucking kidding me?!" Ron asked, slipping to anger. You know what kind of hell I've been through all fucking day, and you were worried about bothering me?"

"I told Erica to try calling you when we didn't hear back from you, but like she said, she didn't want to bother you. And I don't have your new phone number in my phone. Only Erica has it," Kendra said, throwing Erica under the bus.

"That was stupid of you, Erica. You need to use some fucking common sense sometimes. Dumb women are a huge turn off for me, so keep that in mind. I've lost a whole day that I can't get back, and all because you were worried about bothering me. That was really stupid," he yelled.

Erica fought to hold back her tears, while Kendra fought to hold in her laugh.

"Is there anything I can do to make you feel better?" Kendra asked, hoping to score some brownie points.

"No! You ladies get dressed and go to a movie or something. I'll be staying in a different room tonight."

Now it was Kendra who wanted to cry. The constant rejection was becoming more than she wanted to deal with. A big part of her wanted to turn away from the deal, but she needed what Ron had to offer.

"Cool!" Kendra answered, trying to sound chipper.

Erica, on the other hand, was unable to hold back her tears.

Kendra could hardly believe her ears when Ron went over to hug Erica and told her, "Fine, Kendra can go to the movies with Angela and Tonjenae, while you and I spend a peaceful, quiet night together. I don't need you all upset with my baby," he said with a smile before kissing her.

Kendra cleared her throat to signal Erica to back off before she started talking. Erica got the hint.

"I appreciate it, but I really would love to go to a movie. I haven't been in forever. We only watch bootleg videos. Not only that, you have other children to create," she said, faking being upbeat.

"That's exactly why I love you so much. You have been so selfless and always willing to do whatever you can to make me happy," he expressed, kissing her again. "Still, I'd rather just relax with you tonight. These past few days have been very stressful. I can deal with the others tomorrow. Hopefully, we'll be back at the house tomorrow, so we'll have forever after that."

On the brink of telling Ron to go fuck himself, Kendra excused herself to the bathroom. Tired of feeling like an afterthought, she had considered getting pregnant and then going to get an abortion after taking his money, just so she wouldn't have to deal with him afterwards. She was even more tired of doing whatever he wanted to help him keep Erica sexually pleased.

She came out of the bathroom just in time to see the pair on the verge of sex. Ron was peeling off his clothes, and Erica was already nude on the bed. Kendra quietly went back into the bathroom, and this time, she did cry. She realized the arrangement was more difficult to deal with than she thought. She also realized a night away from Ron and Erica was just what she needed for her own sanity.

21

A month had gone by, the house was mostly fixed up, and the women were all moved in and settled. Everything had been going just about perfect with Ron's plan. All the ladies except Kendra were pregnant. He had been spending extra time trying to get her pregnant. He was going to give her only a few more weeks before booting her out and finding a replacement for her. He'd been putting so much time into trying to please the nine ladies, who he nicknamed his "bunnies", that he hardly spent any time at his office.

He hadn't heard from any of his children since his last conversation with them when he was trying to get the combination to his safe. He often amused himself with thoughts of defeating Ava in the war that she declared. He still wanted to find out about the man she was with in Miami so he could crush that guy. Deep down, he wanted his wife to come crawling back, because he'd been finding that life without her was difficult. He hadn't realized how many things she stayed on top of. He didn't know how the utility bills, taxes, insurance, mortgage, lawn and pool service, or any of that stuff worked.

When Ron first met Ava over thirty-one years ago, he was still renting an expensive apartment in Manhattan and didn't buy a house in Jersey until his wedding. Aside from the son she already had, Ava pushed to get custody of Shara, and based on their bond, no one would have ever known Ava didn't birth Shara. Ava was overprotective of Shara, just as much as she was with Jeremy. That's how much Shara clung to and loved Ava. Shortly after their marriage, Ava convinced Ron that it made better economic sense to relocate his company to New

Jersey as opposed to New York City. At that time, he loved Ava with everything inside of him because she helped to bring him back from the brink of business failure and stood by him in his darkest days. As such, he wanted her to feel like a partner in his life in every way and therefore gave her part ownership of his company. Even the employees adored Ava. She treated everyone as if they were friends and family, which created deep-rooted loyalty and high productivity for the company. After the birth of Eve, Ava took more of a background role but still managed to juggle the children, the business, the home, and her frisky husband. Sadly, that is also when Ron's sexual attention span veered off course, and it hadn't been right since. Despite it all, his love for his wife continued to grow, and he often felt like the luckiest man on the planet to have Ava as his wife.

The thought of her being easily able to run off with another man was exceptionally disturbing to Ron. She blocked him on social media, but he was able to look on Eve's page. That's where he saw three sexy photos, posted by Eve, of Ava in Miami. Eve wanted everyone to know her mother still had it going on. One photo was of Ava flanked by three younger looking, muscular, handsome men. Another was of her playing in the turquoise water, and the third, she was stretched out on a beach lounge chair. The pictures were dated around the time he was in the hospital. He hoped the story of her being in Miami with some man was a lie but seeing her looking happier than ever crushed his spirits. He was also bothered by the fact that Eve seemed to be celebrating his wife's infidelity by bragging on her social media page and flaunting Ava's seemingly promiscuous behaviors. This was contradicting of when she came to the hospital pretending to be upset that their mother had run off with another man. Sadly, all his other children had blocked him, as well. So, he couldn't view any of their pages for additional information.

Dealing with a bunch of young girls proved to be difficult at times for Ron, who was used to holding intelligent, thought-provoking conversations with Ava, their couple-friends, and even their own children. However, since the separation, everyone chose to maintain their alliance with Ava, not him. Even the employees in the office looked at him with disdain, and he couldn't seem to get answers when asking any questions.

While Ava was adamant about staying in Jersey, Ron was led to Atlanta by his hormones. Atlanta seemed to offer a wealth of voluptuous women to choose from, and that was Ron's primary focus when he uprooted his business, his wife and their children almost ten years ago. Eve was about to attend Spellman College; Jeremy and Shara were already living their lives; and Ava hated winters. All of those things made his sell a lot easier. Ava refused to go if Ron planned to terminate any New Jersey employee. That's when he allowed her and Jeremy to purchase the Jersey company, and Jeremy ultimately converted it into a very successful defense contracting company, utilizing all of the original employees. When each of the kids became of age, they were automatically given stock in the company because Ron had always anticipated that they would eventually take over running the company after college.

Ariana showed the most interest in working for the company, but that was more to help out her mother, who seemed stretched to capacity. Ariana spent her entire life being told how beautiful she was and would always be questioned about being a model. She received her Bachelor's in business to appease her father, but with her mother's blessing, she received her Master's in Theater & Fine Arts, which is where her passion lie.

Rashaun spent his high school years trying to recreate Jersey in Atlanta. He was always trying to plan and promote some hype event. Since he also liked basketball, he headed to Georgetown for college; his mother gave her blessings while his father forbade. He only played one year before deciding to focus on doing party-type events, as well as public speaking events. With Ava's maternal assistance and strategic business development knowledge, Rashaun was able to create a very successful brand. Additionally, he conducted business seminars on Technology in Business, whereas Jeremy was able to help shape the path for him based on his own expertise.

Ron always looked at Rashaun as competition for Ava's affection. That was mainly because Ron created a job for some woman while Ava was pregnant with Rashaun, then decided to have an affair with the woman, and was with that woman when Ava went into labor, which almost resulted in him missing the birth of his son. She called Ava saying she was sending him on his way for the birth of their first son together… with her pussy still on his lips. Five kids deep, Ava was ready to walk away from Ron, and in an act of desperation to get her to stay, he signed over a majority of the ownership of his company to prove to Ava how dedicated he would be from then on. So, Ava stayed, and the wolf tried to maintain his sheep image for as long as he could. More importantly, he learned never to deal with a trouble-making or demanding woman, such as the one who had called Ava at the hospital to let her know she had just finished fucking Ron. The woman also added that she was going to abort the baby she was carrying. Ron swore the woman was never pregnant. Nonetheless, Ava knew she would never give Ron another child and terminated her ability to do so, which angered Ron when he found out because he wanted more children.

Ron tended to forget that he was no longer a major shareholder to his own company. Never wanting to emasculate her husband, that's what Ava allowed him to continue thinking. With Ron getting up in age and getting scattered in the brain, Ava had been working on their exit strategy from the business for a while, and they allowed staff to become shareholders in the company. The time when Ron agreed to that plan was around the same time that yet another of his women decided to challenge Ava for her husband. The woman told Ava that the only reason he stayed was because Ava would get half of everything. Ron swore it was all a lie and decided to buy the eleven-bedroom mansion in Ava's name on the heels of the other woman's allegation. He didn't originally set out to put the house in Ava's name, but he wanted to buy the new home to help her get over his latest escapade, while claiming it would be for the grandchildren they would have one day.

A little over three years later, Ron started making claims of Ava trying to get half of everything, which let Ava know the woman in the past had been telling the truth…not that she ever doubted her. He was becoming senile since he couldn't remember that he barely owned anything anymore. Because of that affair, the employee distribution of company shares took more ownership away from him without him realizing it since it was Ava who worked tirelessly with the attorneys to work out the distribution arrangement Ron trusted his wife to handle. But, the main reason he wasn't involved was that he was already out scouting his next piece of young ass that he could tame once his wife got over the previous escapade.

Wanting a night away from the ladies, Ron decided to rent a room at the same Marriott where he first met the ladies. He wanted to go to a cigar bar on the south end of Atlanta, have a few cocktails, and perhaps engage in some grownup conversations with people who were older than his bunnies.

It was already September, and the weather had been fickle…cool some evenings, blazing hot on others. Ron was glad for the cooler evening because he wanted to dress in one of his new suits and not be too hot. He had seen his barber earlier in the day, and he was quite pleased at his reflection. Although he had yet to receive his personal credit cards that he reordered, he still had two of the company credit cards, a thousand dollars in cash in his wallet, and another two thousand dollars stashed in his bag in the hotel. He knew he was going to have a great night.

At the cigar bar, he was glad he recognized a few faces. None were actual friends, but just guys to talk to in general. While enjoying his time, he noticed a beautiful, but familiar face continually staring at him. He took that as an invitation, first sending her a drink and then going over.

"I know this sounds like a pickup line, but you look very familiar," he said.

She smiled and replied, "Yes, it does sound like a corny pickup line, but you look familiar, as well. I've been trying to place your face."

When she smiled, he instantly recognized the cute gap she had between her teeth. "You're a nurse?"

"Yeah. How did you know?" she asked, still trying to place his face.

"I was in the hospital the end of July with the shingles and you came into my room once."

She laughed and acted embarrassed. "Oh, you're that crazy guy with the funky rash that had the nerve to be trying to flirt."

"Guilty!" Ron also laughed. "That darn rash was definitely making me crazy. I promise, if you get to know me, you'll find out I'm a pretty normal guy…whatever that's supposed to mean."

"Hell, they all said you were crazy. They had the nerve to call me from my regular floor and ask if I could apply some cream or ointment on you since the other guy wasn't there that evening. When you pulled your thing out, I knew I had to go."

"Wait. So you're saying the guy wasn't supposed to be rubbing cream on my privates?" Ron asked, getting annoyed.

"Are you serious? I don't know where all you had blisters, but hell, you could have rubbed cream on your own dick." She chuckled at her own comment.

Ron could feel his blood beginning to boil. "Enough about that! I came out to enjoy my evening tonight. So, is it possible to get to know you better? Maybe get your name?"

"Oh, I'm sorry. My name is Chloe, and as you know, I'm a RN at the hospital. Psychiatric patients are typically my specialty. I live in Lithonia. I do have a husband, but he drives trucks all over the country. I'm thirty. Actually, just celebrated the big 3-0 two weeks ago…and I don't know what else to tell you."

"Happy belated birthday to you, Chloe. Not sure if you remember, but my name is Ron. I won't tell you how old I am just yet because I don't want to scare you off. I own Johnson, Incorporated, which is located in Midtown. I live in Roswell. Unfortunately, but fortunately, I'm currently separated," he said, looking her body up and down, making it known he was interested. "You're a very beautiful lady. I noticed that even when I was going crazy in the hospital."

She showed her gap when she smiled. "Thank you."

"And that gap…I love it. It is so sexy," he added.

"Uh! You think so? I hate it. I said one day I'm going to have enough money to get it fixed."

"I really like it. You should leave it."

"Even my husband's always making fun about it. He calls me Alfalfa from the *Little Rascals*." She faintly laughed, letting Ron know she didn't like the teasing.

"That's really mean. He shouldn't say stuff like that. He should adore every single thing about you."

"Shoot, that's why I'm glad he stays gone so much. I don't have to be bothered with his mouth."

Ron frowned. "Doesn't sound like much of a marriage. How long have you been together?"

"We've been together almost a year and a half but have been married for a little over a year. June made a year."

"Okay, wow! You married quickly."

She rolled her eyes up toward the ceiling. "Too quickly. He came and stayed with me for a night and never left. At the time, he didn't even have a job and was staying with family. When he got the truck driving job, he insisted we go to the courthouse to get married. Went down to DeKalb County and got married. The way things be with trying to find a man here, I figured I better get a husband while I could."

"Any children?"

"My husband has seven kids. I only knew about one before we married. Then he started springing the others on me one by one, with that 'Oh, I thought I told you' mess. All of his pay gets taken by child support, so it's like I have to take care of everything concerning the household."

"That's really too bad. You're such a beautiful woman and deserve to be happy, not have to settle. What does your family have to say about it all?"

Chloe laughed. "Please! They were the main ones talking about I better grab hold of that man while I could. My momma is on her third marriage. My younger sister is married. I had been single for so long, pushing thirty, that I got desperate and married the first man who asked. I used to want a baby, but when I found out about his seven kids, two of them being babies, I changed my mind. One of those babies was born after we were married, but he got the girl pregnant before we got together. The other baby was born a month before we got married, but I didn't know anything about her either. He has a four-year-old, six-year-old, two eight-year-olds, and a twelve-year-old, all by different mothers."

"Oh my! That's crazy. I never understood why people make children they can't afford to take care of."

"Exactly! That's the main reason why I don't want to have his baby," she responded, taking a sip of her drink.

"You ever think about divorcing him and perhaps finding someone better?"

"Every now and again, I go out, like I am tonight, just to see what I'm missing. But, every man that approaches me either already has a woman at home or is just coming out of a marriage and not looking for anything serious, which I'm sure is your story, as well."

"Yeah, I guess. I take it that dating must be difficult for women in Atlanta, huh?"

She laughed. "That would be putting it mildly."

"My wife didn't seem to have any problem moving on, which made me wonder."

"Ooh, I'm sorry to hear that," Chloe said, placing her hand over Ron's hand out of concern. "Was your separation around the time you were in the hospital? 'Cause that would explain what had you going crazy."

"Those shingles had me going crazy. Thought I'd lose my mind."

"Shingles usually come from excessive stress."

"Well, then yes, that was the same time I learned my wife took off to Miami with another man."

"That's messed up. Even worse, they put you on a 51-50, when she should have been the one locked up."

"A 51-50? What's that? I remember hearing that before."

"An involuntary psych hold."

"You must be mistaken. My personal doctor arranged my admission into isolation because I was covered from head to toe in a shingles rash."

"Oh! I could be wrong. I thought it was a psych hold, but I do remember them saying you were contagious and had to be isolated. I don't know. They could have put you in the other building for that, though."

"Is the other building highly populated? My doctor told me that they wanted to keep me from heavy population because of my CEO status, said he didn't want to risk people bothering me and perhaps catching what I had."

"Oh well, I guess that makes sense. It does get crazy over there, but they have a lot of celebrities who are hospitalized there all the time," she answered, still skeptical about his treatment. "I know they were saying you had shingles, but I asked them if it could possibly be something else. It reminded me of poison ivy."

Ron laughed. "I wish! At one point, it got worse after almost being cleared up. I had to stay fifteen days in the hospital for that shit."

"Wow! That's horrible. Yeah, that definitely sounds like shingles. Anyhow, I'm glad you're all better now. I'm about ready to get up out of here and maybe go find some dinner or something."

Ron smiled. "Well, I have yet to eat. Maybe you wouldn't mind joining me. I'm not trying to be too forward or anything.

I have a room over at the Marriott, and they have some great food at the restaurant there."

She flirted with a closed lip smile, letting him know she'd be down to do whatever he wanted. "Sure. I'll follow you there. I don't want to leave my car down here."

"Great!"

Ron escorted Chloe to the exit after settling his tab, making sure all the other guys were checking them out as they left together.

22

Ron practically had Chloe's clothes off while in the elevator heading up to his room after dinner. Her kisses were desperate, letting him know that despite her being married, it had been a long time since she'd been fulfilled. She literally had to hold her blouse to her bosom to cover herself as they made their way from the elevator to his room. Even Ron's pants were already open.

Once inside the room, clothes and shoes were flying everywhere. His fingers slid their way inside Chloe's soaking pussy. She moaned loudly as if cumming on contact, and the pair had only made it to right inside the door. She aggressively but sensually massaged his tool, causing it to grow harder and longer. That in itself turned her on.

As soon as they made it to another wall further into the room, he spun her around and pushed up inside of her. She screamed out for the world to hear, and his grunts were equally telling as he pounded her from behind. When his leg cramped, he stopped long enough to guide her to the bed, where he laid down on his back for her to climb on top of him. As she skillfully rotated her pelvis and grinded against his, with him fully inserted inside of her, he found himself interchangeably reflecting on various magical moments with each of his bunnies. He found himself comparing each. Chloe functioned as if she were in full control, not waiting to be given any directions. Over and over again, she'd take Ron to the brink of an explosion but would stop it to prolong him. That was a skill she strongly possessed over the others, who seemed hell-bent on doing what they needed to do to get him to a quicker climax.

Chloe managed to garner Ron's total and undivided attention. That made him more excited about bringing her to an ultimate explosion.

He flipped her on her back and decided to play her game, driving her insane. She clawed at his back and arms, but it didn't concern him one bit, as he didn't have to worry about Ava seeing the marks. From time to time, he'd pull out just to devour her thick protrusive areolas, then he'd thrust back up inside of her. Each time he would pull his dick out, he'd insert fingers inside to feel her gushing. He flipped her on her stomach and onto her knees, kissing each ass cheek before burying his face between them to suck up some of the wetness. She buried her face in the pillow, but then lifted it and screamed from deep in her throat. When he had enough, he reentered her from behind. As he pounded her, he entertained himself by watching his tool disappear inside of her and reappear with gobs of her wetness on it. Her screams were causing him to lose control in addition to the hand she stretched in between her legs to massage his testicles.

His pace increased, signaling that he was reaching his breaking point. He even began speaking in tongues. That turned her on more, causing her to match his pace until they finally exploded together. Ron held her around her waist for dear life as the last of his ejaculation shot through her, in possible search for an egg to fertilize. He never once stopped to ask if she was on protection. Then the pair collapsed on the bed to catch their breath.

After a few minutes, Ron got up to use the bathroom while Chloe reached for the remote to turn on the television. There was a light knock at the door. He chuckled to himself, thinking it was probably security telling them to keep the noise down. He wrapped a towel around his waist to answer the door. Chloe didn't hear the knock because of the television and because the door was near the bathroom.

Ron opened the door with a huge smile, but it wasn't security. It was a thuggish looking, muscular guy who stood a hair taller than Ron at six-foot-one.

"You in here fucking my wife?!" the guy yelled, busting into the room and pushing Ron down in the process. "Chloe, get your ass up, you whore! Everybody tried to tell me you were playing my ass while I'm on the road. I didn't want to believe that shit."

Chloe tried to jump up off of the bed, but the man already had a hold of her hair. Unsure of what to do, Ron charged at the guy. The only thing he remembered before everything went black was a fist coming towards his face.

When he came to, everything was blurry. He didn't have to see in order to know his entire body, including his groin area, had suffered a severe beating. It was hard for him to breathe as he laid naked on the floor. He was unable to get up but managed to crawl to the hotel phone, pull it off the desk, and call the front desk for an ambulance. He also pulled a cover from the bed and wrapped it around him because he didn't want to be found naked. By the time someone arrived to the room, he was drifting in and out of consciousness. He didn't even recall his transport to the hospital.

*****

Ron woke up in ICU. He wasn't sure if he was dreaming when he saw an angelic version of his wife sitting in a chair across the room, watching him with disgust.

"Ava? Ava, is that you, darling?" he whispered, struggling to speak.

"Yes, Ron, it's me. It's not a dream or the meds."

"Oh, baby! Thank you for coming. I'm so lost without you. I need you. Ava, do you hear me? I need you. I can't live without you," he cried.

"Ron, you have a collapsed lung. Save your breath. We'll talk later when you get better."

"Who called you? How did you know I was here?"

"The hospital called me. They weren't sure if you'd pull

through. I'm not a total monster, Ron. I'll still care about your well-being even if we're no longer married."

"Oh, Ava, you do still love me. We belong together."

Ava rolled her eyes, not quite in the mood to crush him just yet.

"What happened? How did I end up here?" he asked.

She rolled her eyes again. "Apparently, one of the hos you picked up last night must have belonged to somebody else, and they set your ass up. The video showed them leaving the room together, carrying your bag and leaving you with nothing. Not even your underwear."

"She wasn't in on it. I remember him grabbing her by the hair when she tried to run."

"Oh, so now you remember, huh? That selective amnesia," Ava asked dryly. "Funny, the video shows her carrying your bag out of your room, and I'm guessing that was your phone, wallet, and watch he had in his hands," she sarcastically added. "You're going to need some clothes to leave the hospital. You currently have nothing but that gown you're wearing."

"How long will I be here?"

"Probably a few days. It's not like you're some young guy. You'll take longer to heal. You had to have three stitches under your eye. Your right lung is partially collapsed. You have blood in your eye and in your urine. Your wrist is broken. Your heart rate is all over the place, and umm, yeah, you pretty much got fucked up. You literally got the shit beat out of you, since they said they found some poop on the floor and thought you might have had a stroke. But, you didn't." Ava fought herself to keep from laughing. She would save her laughter for later when he was out of danger and doing better. "Anyhow, I have things to do. I have to get going."

"Please, Ava, don't leave me. You're my everything."

"Later, Ron. Get better!"

"I'll forgive you for cheating on me. I don't care. I love and need you."

She spun around to face him. "You're going to do what?

Forgive me?" she asked, half tempted to snatch his oxygen from him.

"Baby, I forgave you with the Rashaun affair, and I don't care now. We belong together, Ava."

"Rashaun affair?" she asked, getting even more annoyed. "He's your fucking son, you idiot. I didn't cheat. That was you laid up with a bitch, talking about replacing me while I was laying up there giving birth to your son. Man, fuck you! You deserved to have your ass beat for a change. I always knew it would only be a matter of time before someone got your ass. I'll get you some clothes dropped off, and then I'm washing my hands of you, you delusional old fart!"

"Please, Ava, I'm sorry. I'm just a stupid old fool. I don't know what I'm talking about. I'm all confused right now. Don't be angry with me. Please," he sobbed.

Ava turned away to hide her pain. Despite all the stupid things he'd done, she loved him and hated seeing him like that. Her kids refused to visit him once they learned he had been beaten as a result of being in a hotel with a different woman other than the ones in their home.

"I have to go, Ron," she said without facing him, then hurried out of his hospital room.

23

Ava and Ariana couldn't believe their eyes when they let themselves inside the house to get clothing to take to Ron in the hospital. Ariana didn't want to get anything for her father nor did she want her mother helping him, but she felt compelled to accompany her mother for safety, as well as to be nosey.

"Who are you, and why are you just walking into our house like you own the place?" Kennedy asked when she noticed Ava and Ariana as she was walking by, heading to another room.

Ariana quickly whipped out her phone and held her nose as she recorded the nasty scene of a bunch of pregnant, juvenile-looking girls walking around the filthy house butt naked and wearing only stilettos. The air wreaked of funky pussy odor.

"Like I own the place?" Ava laughed. "Yeah, I actually do own it, and you better watch your tone with me before I put you out right this second."

"This is Ron's house," Toni chimed in.

"Bitch, go put some fucking clothes on! Y'all a bunch of nasty hos. And I dare you to say something else to me or my mother."

Some of the other girls gathered amongst themselves as Ava and Ariana continued to walk around and assess the mess.

"What's going on?" Kendra asked.

"That's his wife. I remember seeing her picture," Erica answered. "Ron said you don't live here anymore. He said this is his house and you can't put us out."

The others all cosigned.

"Oh my God! Momma, please let's just get the hell out of

here. I told you not to help his ass, getting clothes for him," Ariana said, trying to grab her mother's arm to leave.

"Wait, Ari. I want to ask them something."

Ariana sucked her teeth and rolled her eyes but waited while still recording the nude women.

"Aren't you all teenagers? Are your mothers aware that you have thrown your lives away like this? And the three of you look like sisters. Are you?" Ava asked, pointing to Sherita, Shirleen, and Sherrell.

"Our mother is fine with it because it's our chance to have a better life. We're all legal, so we don't need our mothers' permission," Kendra answered.

"A better life? Does he require that you all walk around naked?"

"I ain't ashamed of my body. I don't have to hide it, and he likes it that way," Angela replied with pride.

"So, let me get this right. All seven…eight…nine of you are carrying my husband's baby and don't see anything wrong with that? He's an old man. Probably your grandfather's age. How much longer do you think he's going to be around? And for the sake of argument, let's just say he survives another hundred years. Some of you are barely showing, and he's already off with other women."

"Ron's not interested in being with other women. He only went out last night to hang with guy friends," Erica defended.

Ava cracked up laughing. "Sorry, sweetie, but my husband has no *guy* friends. None. And the fact that I came here to pick up some clothes to take to him in the hospital because someone beat the literal shit out of his ass for screwing their woman and then robbed him… If that don't tell you that you're nothing more than a hiccup for him–"

"And trust me, I'm his daughter, so I know firsthand," Ariana added, cutting her mother off.

"You all are going to have to leave this house within a month. Where will you go? He doesn't have shit. What do you think he can do for you?" Ava asked.

"Why do we have to leave if this is Ron's house? We're having his baby, and he said we can be here," Erica argued.

"I guess you'll have to wait and see. You should also know that my husband just finished begging for us to be back together, saying you all were nothing more than a phase. But, I can promise you that after seeing this nasty, funky, disgusting sight, you don't ever have to worry about me taking him away from you. Oh, and I should also let you know that he's not the least bit serious about any of you. You all were nothing more than a plot to try to hurt me, and trust, looking at his pathetic ass laying up in that hospital, talking about he needs me and can't live without me…" Ava laughed. "…he ain't hurting no one but himself and put a bunch of poor, unsuspecting teenagers, who are so desperate for a come up, in the crossfire."

"I'm not a teenager. I'm twenty-four," Sherita said like that made a difference.

Ava looked at her as if she were stupid. "For them, I can sympathize because they are so young and don't know any better than trying to play house with a dirty old man who they thought had something that would make their lives betters. But you? You're a special kind of fool. It wouldn't surprise me if you're the one who brought the others into this three-ring circus… Nine-ring circus is more like it."

"Momma, that's the girl, Sherita…the one he was having sex with in his office on video," Ariana pointed out.

Ava looked carefully at Sherita and then at Shirleen, who closely resembled her.

"Yes. Yes, it is." Ava laughed again. "Well, I have nothing left to say or do here. I think I'll let my husband's pack of whores do the good deed and take his clothes to the hospital. He's in Atlanta Medical South. You handle it the best way you can, Miss Sherita." Ava turned to walk away.

"Oh my goodness! He's really in the hospital," Tonjenae finally spoke up, most upset.

Ava turned back when she heard Tonjenae. "Oh, you must be the one who actually cares about him and not what he can do for you. You're the only one who seems bothered about him being in the hospital."

"I care," Erica said, rolling her eyes.

"Whatever! Who gives a shit? Then go see the dying old man. Oh yeah, that's right," she said, snapping her fingers. "You're not his wife, so they won't let you in his room. Guess you'll just have to sit here and wait to see what will happen. Well, at least until the thirty-day eviction takes effect."

After Ava and Ariana left, the girls became frantic as they argued amongst themselves. When they tried to call the hospital, they were given no information because they weren't immediate family. When they lied and said they were, the hospital staff asked for a password, which no one knew.

The following day, the entire household was served with an eviction order to vacate the premises within thirty days.

24

"You must've really pissed off a lot of people for no one to have come see about you since your wife, and that was a week ago," the obnoxious nurse said as she wheeled Ron into the elevator, transporting him to a taxi during his discharge. "Good thing they were able to find you some clothes that fit you out of the donation box. I'm also surprised the hospital gave you a taxi voucher to get all the way back to Roswell. They typically just give enough for the bus to go up the street."

The more the older woman spoke, the closer Ron came to telling her to shut the fuck up. He was already disturbed by Ava's latest disappearing act after having poured out his heart to her yet again. He lost his phone and again had no way of calling one of his bunnies. He was pissed that collectively, they were all too stupid to track him down. He was angered that he couldn't even go get his car from the hotel because he had no key. Also, once again, he was without ID, but at least this time, he knew he had an extra license at home. He didn't have any keys to go to his office and get some money. He wasn't even sure how much he had left in his safe. Since his business credit cards were stolen along with his ID, he'd have to inform the office staff to cancel those cards and order new ones. Yeah, he was pissed.

"Tonjenae!" he yelled out when they were approaching the exit and he saw her standing alone looking lost.

She sobbed the second she spotted him and went running to hug him tightly. "Oh my God! You're alive!"

She cried as she examined all of the visible damage to his face and the cast on his arm.

"What are you doing here? How long have you been standing there waiting?" he asked, happier than ever to see her.

"Your wife told us that you were here, but they wouldn't let us call or see you because we're not your family. Since I knew you were here, I drove down here each day, hoping to catch you leaving so I could take you home." She held up a small duffle bag. "I even brought clothes for you. I stopped and bought a new phone for you, too. I had no way of getting it to you, though. No one would deliver it."

He was beyond impressed with Tonjenae in that moment.

"No one else came with you?" he asked, looking around.

She rolled her eyes and shook her head, obviously disgusted with the others.

Wearing some awful-looking clothes, Ron stood from the wheelchair and turned to the nurse, letting her know he would no longer be needing her services or the taxi. The nurse seemed offended as she strolled away. Ron took the bag from Tonjenae to go find a men's room to change clothes. Tonjenae cried some more while Ron was in the men's room. When he came out, he noticed that she kept trying to stop her flow of tears. He went over to her and held her tightly as she unleashed.

Once in the car, Ron said, "I know I must look pretty bad. You should have seen me a few days ago. I actually look pretty good right now compared to then," he joked. "Tonjenae, before things get too hectic, I want you to know how much I love and appreciate you. I can't begin to express how much what you've done means to me. Thank you."

He reached over for a quick kiss while the light was red.

"I think I would have died had I seen you in worse shape. The thought of you hurt and alone..." She choked up, and the tears formed again. "I hate everything you've been through already, and now things are about to get even worse."

"How so?" he asked, half not really wanting to know.

"Sherita's momma, my Aunt Shirley, has been trying to get you locked up. She's accusing you of brainwashing us and having a cult. Not only that, but the sheriff came and served all of us eviction papers the day after your wife came and told us that we had thirty days to be out of the house. The other girls are only worried about themselves. Kendra was about to leave, but then she came up pregnant. When Kendra had plans to go, she blabbed that Erica might be pregnant by Bishop Rogers. He's the slimy, pedophile preacher that sleeps with the young girls in the neighborhood. Everybody knows to go to him when they need money, and Erica went there when you were in the hospital a few months ago. Next thing, she says she's pregnant. Now, we're all wondering who the daddy is."

Ron was stunned. He didn't know what was most disturbing. *Erica? Erica?* He would have never thought such about her, but he clearly recalled his encounter with the seemingly overly possessive bishop.

Wait! An eviction? The insanity, he thought.

Sherita's mother was the least of his concerns. He was still too stunned by the news about Erica and his wife's attempt to have him thrown out of his home.

"How well do you know this bishop, and what do you know about his reputation?" Ron pressed.

Tonjenae was embarrassed to answer. "Trust me, I and every girl in Griffin knows from personal experience. Depending on how developed the girl is, he's been known to be with girls who are only thirteen or fourteen years old. It's crazy, because girls somehow know to go see him if they are in need of money or something. It's not like he goes seeking them out."

"Everyone knows this man is sleeping with little girls, and he's not in jail?" Ron asked.

"Nope. No one complains. It's like the normal thing around there. Mr. Fredricks is another one who likes to touch teenaged girls. Most of the time, he don't be having sex with them. He just be touching on them inside his store. In exchange, he lets them have whatever they want in the store. He also has a little bed in the back. I heard some girls be going back there with him."

"Erica, also?" Ron asked, not wanting to believe it.

"Shoot yeah! I saw her coming out one time after the store was closed in the middle of the day. Everybody be knowing stuff around there."

"Have you?"

Tonjenae shrugged, not wanting to have to admit it but not wanting to lie either.

"Yeah, but I ain't never go in the back."

"This is so disturbing to hear."

"Kendra also said Erica sleeps with her momma's boyfriend, and that's why she can't stay with her momma no more. She said she saw the boyfriend coming out of Erica's place in the middle of the night while you were in the hospital, and Erica didn't even deny it. Not only that, but she let some boys run a train on her. Kendra's one to talk, though, 'cause everybody knows dudes be running trains on her all the time. Especially when she be braiding their heads."

Ron felt a sinking in the pit of his stomach. He was also disturbed about being forever tied to a bunch of damaged girls. He didn't want to hear any more about them.

"So what about this eviction you mentioned? You said it came from my wife? Does she not know that's my house and she can't evict me?" He laughed.

"She told us it was her house, and we'd have thirty days to be out of it. The next day, the sheriff came and served the papers."

"My wife is just blowing smoke and trying to scare you. Nothing to worry about."

"She said you told her that you wanted to be back with her. Is that what you want?"

Ron's jaw tightened, pretty much letting Tonjenae know it was true.

"Not really. I'll be honest, though. Sometimes it's hard being without her because she always handled everything. I hadn't realized how easy she made my life until now. She's been the backbone of my existence for thirty-one years. Now,

I'm trying to figure out how to stand on my own, and it's kind of hard. I guess it's like when a kid first leaves his parents' home. Eventually, he makes out okay, but not without a few bumps and bruises first."

"I can understand," Tonjenae said, reaching over to hold Ron's hand, giving him a much-needed sense of security.

He raised her hand to his lips and kissed it. They rode the rest of the way in silence.

When they arrived to the house, everyone seemed so happy to see him. Erica even cried, hugging him the longest. He was unimpressed, though.

"I have one question for you all. Why was Tonji alone?"

"We didn't think you wanted us going off all over Atlanta. We thought you'd be mad," Sherrell answered when none of the others spoke up.

"No, what makes me angry is that none of you had sense enough to go with her to make sure she was okay. I understand my wife told you to bring me clothes to the hospital, but only one person in this house even considered that I needed those clothes or even a way from the fucking hospital. Every one of you are pathetic. Sherita, you're the oldest and know your way around Atlanta. I definitely would expect more common sense from you."

The women looked afraid of Ron.

"All of you, get the fuck out of my face. Sherita, you and Shirleen can go to the store to get my prescription filled," he said handing them the papers. "I'm going to my room to relax. Tonji, I'd like for you to keep me company," he said, then walked off slowly as he struggled to make it to his bedroom.

Tonjenae's feelings were hurt at first when he yelled at them, but she felt much better when he chose her to go with him to his bedroom.

After resting for a while, he summoned Sherrell, Kendra, and Erica into his room to deal with the things Tonjenae had told him.

"First, I'll deal with you, Sherrell. Do you feel you are here against your will?"

She looked offended. "No! Absolutely not! I love it here."

"Do you feel I forced you to get pregnant or took advantage of you sexually?"

"No," she answered, her face still twisted.

"I understand your mother is trying to have me locked up for taking advantage of you all. Where did she get that notion? Sherita's twenty-four and Shirleen is now twenty-one. You're the youngest, so why does she think you are here against your will?"

"I swear I don't know why she's doing that. I figured she was mad about us leaving her, but we still help her with the bills from the money you gave us. I don't know why she's mad," Sherrell pled, on the verge of tears.

"Their momma is just stupid," Kendra spoke up. "My momma told me that Miss Shirley tried to go to the police, but they said she couldn't do anything because we're all grown. So, she started saying she was going to the news, but my momma got mad at her and told her that she better not. My momma's willing to stand up for you if need be. Shoot, Miss Shirley was like fifteen or sixteen when Sherita was born, so she ain't got room to talk about no one. She ain't even forty yet. She's just looking for a payday."

"Speaking of payday, I understand you're finally pregnant, huh?" he asked Kendra.

Grinning, she patted her still flat belly.

"Don't get too happy too soon. Kendra, I also understand you've been withholding some very important information from me concerning Erica and the bishop?"

Both Erica and Kendra looked shocked.

"Actually," he continued, "I've learned quite a bit about the bishop fucking each of you. Not only that, but y'all let the neighborhood boys and the man in the store do whatever to you. What's wrong with you? Are you really that fucked up?"

Growing bold, Kendra asked, "What's the difference from what we do with you? We have a need; y'all give us what we need; and we do whatever to get whatever it is we need."

Kendra's words left Ron feeling like a piece of shit.

"So, you all are prostitutes. Is that what you're telling me?" he yelled, trying to regain control of the conversation.

She remained silent.

"I don't be with him like that anymore. I only did it a couple of times when I was like fourteen, but I hated it and never went back," Sherrell confessed. "Same with Toni. Toni ain't been with him since she was like fifteen. He's fat, ugly, and disgusting. He used to make me feel uncomfortable, like you were doing something you didn't wanna do. I don't feel like that with you. I *want* to be with you."

That made Ron feel a little better, but still, he had Erica to deal with. So, he returned his attention back to her.

"When were you going to let me know you might be carrying another man's baby?"

"I swear, Ron, this is your baby. I'm one thousand percent sure."

"There's no such thing as one thousand percent, so does that mean you're lying?"

"I'm not lying. I'll give you the money back to prove I'm not lying to you, and you can give it to me when I have the baby and prove it's yours."

"You slept with the bishop that night he told me you went to see him?" Ron said more as a statement than a question.

"I swear he is not the father. My lights got turned off, and I was desperate. I couldn't get in touch with you, and I didn't know what else to do."

"You're close with your mother. Why didn't you ask her for help? Better yet, what happened to all the money I had given you? I was giving you two to three hundred dollars each time I saw you."

"I had to pay my rent. I don't know. I just got behind on everything."

"You had a job when I met you, and you told me that your rent was less than four hundred dollars per month. The place was so tiny, a single candle would have lit up the entire place. You had a thousand dollars left on your car payment, and I paid that over the phone to the finance company. Erica, you are so full of shit. You fucked that man because you wanted to fuck him, and you've been fucking him for many years. Am I correct?"

Erica covered her face in shame as she cried, then yelled out, "I know who the father of my baby is! You are! You're the only one I was with. I was seeing you almost every other day until you went in the hospital."

"And when I went in the hospital, I called you and you knew where I was at. Yet, this is the bullshit you do while I was in the hospital worried sick about if you were also sick? But, the bishop's dick wasn't enough for you. You were fucking your mother's boyfriend, as well, and all while supposedly carrying my child." Ron waved his hand. "Get the fuck away from me. You disgust me. You, too, Kendra, because you should have told me immediately. When was the last time you fucked the good reverend and had a bunch of niggers running trains on your nasty ass?"

Kendra was stunned by his attack on her. She didn't dare tell the truth, especially about having received a finger-fucking from two guys only minutes before running into Ron that day.

"I haven't been with anyone since I met you. Yes, I've done things I regret, but not since I've been with you."

"You know what? I don't even believe you, but I'll give you the money I promised. However, I won't be touching either of you two again."

Erica and Kendra looked crushed to the core.

"Get the fuck out of here, I said!"

They scrambled to leave the room.

"You can leave, as well," he told Sherrell.

She looked like a sad child being dismissed by her parents, and her reaction disturbed Ron.

He asked Tonjenae to give him some time to be by himself. He didn't let her know, but he wanted privacy to cry. He was devastated over the huge mess he had made in each of those young girls' lives. He didn't know what to do. He couldn't tell them to go have an abortion. He wasn't that cruel. He was so deep in poop, he couldn't even remember his purpose for impregnating the women…specifically nine women. Then he remembered the psychic and all she said to him about being a fool that would hang himself. That he definitely agreed with. He wanted to blame her but didn't see how he could. He had to take full ownership of the mess he had made on his own.

He thought about what it was that he continually searched for outside of his marriage, when he already had the perfect woman the entire time. He couldn't blame her for being upset about all the stupid things he'd done, and he couldn't blame her for wanting the women out of their home. The same home he had initially purchased with plans of watching their grandchildren grow up in. Instead, he was now planning on raising nine of his own children in his wife's home without his wife. That thought caused him to think about the eviction papers. He wiped his face and then called for Tonjenae to bring him the papers. As Tonjenae was bringing the papers, Sherita and Shirleen were returning with his pain medication and an envelope that had been delivered by another deputy from the sheriff's office.

"I found this other envelope downstairs near the eviction papers and other mail. I'm not sure when it came," Tonjenae said, handing him a large stack of mail.

"The guy just handed me this for you when I was coming in. I let him know you were in bed and couldn't come downstairs 'cause you just got out of the hospital," Shirleen said, handing him the envelope while Sherita placed his medication on the nightstand.

Ron looked at the overwhelming stack of mail in confusion.

"Could someone bring me some juice for my medicine?" he asked no one in particular.

"I was about to bring you some with your mail, but they

drank it all, and the bottle water is empty," Tonjenae informed him, then cringed.

Ron closed his eyes, ready to blow a gasket. He was exceptionally pissed that Shirleen and Sherita had just spent over an hour waiting in the store for his medicine, but didn't think to bring back anything to drink. He knew Tonjenae was not to blame because she had been spending her days at the hospital waiting for him.

"I don't give a damn which of you go to the store, but you better stock up that kitchen, and you better not ever let something run out again. The rest of you better get this house cleaned up. It looks like a pigsty and it stinks. Tonjenae, I know it's not your fault, but please go to the store with them since it's obvious that they need someone with sense to accompany them."

She smiled. "I can do that. Can I get you something else before I go? I want you to be able to relax until I get back."

Her concern made him smile. "No, thank you. I have lots of mail to go through, and I'll probably take a nap after that. Just give the others the order to clean the house."

Once they left, Ron looked at the eviction notice and saw his name was included. He thought for sure it would only be for the women. His confusion caused him to laugh. Next, he opened the envelope Shirleen had handed him. It was a court summons. He was being sued for five million dollars for Alienation of Affection during the course of committing adultery. He was confused until he kept reading and saw the name Chloe Brown.

"You have got to be fucking kidding me!" he said out loud to himself.

He couldn't believe the man that the police were looking for had the nerve to be trying to sue him for money. He really laughed out loud.

Ron continued going through the mail, hoping to find one of those credit cards he'd been waiting on, but only seeing disconnection notices for all the utilities. Then he saw a notice from a law office, informing him that they were giving him seven days to return the funds stolen from the company by way of two company credit cards and two thousand dollars in cash taken from petty cash. If the debt was not paid in full, they would proceed with filing embezzlement charges against him for theft against the employees, who were all shareholders. The amount of the pre-interest debt shown to date was $307,453.22.

Ron laughed again, thinking he hadn't spent anywhere near that amount. Then he began thinking of all the cash withdrawals, payments to the ladies, refurnishing the house, food, clothing for the women and himself, laptops, expensive pocketbooks, manicures, dinners, and massages. In it all, he hadn't even paid any utility bills or mortgage. He had no idea where he'd get that kind of money. Between Ava and Ariana, they handled the financial dealings for the home and business. He wasn't sure where all the monies from their multiple bank accounts were, and as quick as he received his monthly salary deposits, it was spent almost immediately.

However, the final envelope he opened was the most disturbing yet.

25

"Ava, how could you do this to me? To us? How could you kick me while I was down?"

"Surely you didn't think I would live in the same home with you and your bunch of mistresses, did you? You've disrespected me for the very last time. So now, we're done. You have your freedom to go and do whatever. And you must have been a bigger fool if you thought I'd be the one to assume financial responsibility for your bastard children made with teenagers."

"A fucking divorce! A fucking divorce, though? We could have worked this out. We could have gone to counseling. You didn't even give us a chance to fix things. So we had a little fight. All couples fight. You had no business getting a divorce. You needed my permission. We were supposed to try to work things out before the judge signed a divorce decree. And what's this bullshit about it being uncontested with no spousal support for me?"

"Ron, darling…fool, do you remember, not even a year ago, when YOU drew these papers up with your attorney, which ironically, I thought was a slap in the face to me back then because I felt it should have been me drawing up divorce papers based on all you have done to me. However, based on the terms you outlined, there was nothing for me to quibble about since everything was to my benefit. You do remember it was after yet another of your affairs, the one with the two strippers that you spent five thousand dollars on in one night. You swore it was your last affair, although that also was a lie. To prove you were serious about saving our marriage, you drew up and signed those papers, saying I would deservingly walk away with everything, leaving you with nothing, if you cheated again. Foolishly, I wanted to believe you. I would never have imagined anyone could be so stupid. Well, Ron, I have to admit, that was really, really, really stupid of you to do something like that. Especially knowing you are incapable of keeping your dick in your pants. Do you not remember it all? With those papers in hand, all I had to do is file it with the court whenever I got up the nerve to do so. Thanks to this latest and greatest stunt of yours, I finally found the nerve to end this sham of a marriage. I should have done so the minute you gave them to me, but I wanted to believe you wouldn't be stupid enough to sign over your life and then have the nerve to cheat on me AGAIN after that.

"Additionally, MY company that you THINK you own, you've been voted out of by the shareholders that you stole from, based on your current embezzlement dilemma. And just in case your mind is a little fuzzy about how the company became mine and my children's, that also happened as a result of you trying to prove you wouldn't cheat on me anymore. I would say I must have been a fool to stay with you all these years, but being that I have everything and you have nothing, I think that speaks volumes. Who's the fool now?"

"Ava, I don't have any money to pay that debt. You know I'm a sick man. I have a sickness. I need help, not a divorce. Do you really hate me so much that you'd just take everything and let them lock me up?"

"Do you really love your seven cars more than you love your freedom? You better get to liquidating if you want to keep that butthole a virgin, and trust me, I'm being generous by allowing you to keep those cars since I rightfully can take possession of those, as well. It's included in our divorce, remember?"

"WHAT?! My cars?! Ava, really now? I built this company. I made it what it is today. How can my employees charge me with stealing from the company I built? And what happened to all of our millions of dollars in the bank? I went to the bank a couple of months ago, and they said it was all gone and the credit cards were maxed out."

"No, dear, your cards were cancelled because of your whoredom spending. You took those bitches on a party bus to a steakhouse and wonder where your money is after plopping down almost ten thousand dollars for a fucking dinner alone? Man, you ain't got shit left aside from what's left in that safe of yours and whatever you can get for those cars. Since that reckless activity was at the time I went ahead and filed those divorce papers, I damn sure wasn't going to allow you access to any more of MY funds. Oh no! That would have been mighty dumb of me."

"UGH! Ava, please! I got this guy trying to sue me for five million dollars. I talked to the attorney, and he said the guy might have a legitimate case against me, despite him assaulting and robbing me. Alienation of Affection is not even fucking valid in the state of Georgia anymore."

"Trust me, I am already aware that the law has been abolished, because I would be an even wealthier woman by now," she dryly responded. "However, they're coming from a different angle on your ass. That's what happens when you fuck with other people's wives."

"He gets to scream extreme emotional distress, and I just get screwed."

"What can I tell you, Ron? Your penis has written you a check for that screw that your finances can't cash. Your stupidity is making lawyers wealthy. I'm not sure what else you want me to say or do. You have a problem worse than drugs. You have squandered thousands of dollars per week, and none of it went to a single bill. Yes, I did what I had to do to safeguard the company that you may have started but that I built, while you spent money on whores faster than we could earn it. You still have a couple of shares of interest in the company that may give you some pocket change down the line, but if you don't take steps to erase that debt, I'm sure you will lose your shares along with your freedom."

"Ava, I can't do this alone. I need you."

"Ron, stop! Please! You don't need a wife. You do need help, but I can't help you. You set out to try to destroy me and your own children because you wanted all of us to end up with nothing. Man, that's fucked up on so many levels. And the irony is, Jeremy, Rashaun, and Eve's companies are all in a better financial position than the one you keep bragging about that you started. This company would have been doing so much better if you weren't blowing our money on bitches for almost thirty damn years. But, trust, it'll be doing great from here on out. I have nothing else to say to you, Ron. You're living on borrowed time in my, not your, house. So, I highly suggest you get busy working on finding a home for you and your whores, because y'all won't be in my house for very much longer. I believe you have seventeen days left, so you might want to get off this phone and hop to it. Also, while you keep talking all that shit about needing me and not being able to do whatever alone… Nigga, you got NINE bitches to help you do what you gotta do. So, on that note…Peace!"

"Ava!" Ron screamed through the phone.

"Goodbye, Ron. Good luck with those babies."

She ended the call.

Ron cried like a baby. Tonjenae, who was listening from a distance, came and held him.

When he got quiet, she calmly told him, "Ron, stop worrying. We'll be fine. I found us a five-bedroom house over in Mableton. It's not as fancy as this house, but I think we can at least try to make it work for a few months. Of course, once the babies start coming, we'll have to figure something else out, but let's just deal with one hurdle at a time. I agree with your wife; you need to let maybe two or three of those cars go so you can stay out of prison. Let's focus on moving forward." Tears formed as she choked to continue. "And don't worry about your wife right now. She's hurt and angry, but eventually, she'll come around. Then you two can work things out and be back together as you'd like."

Those words were exceptionally painful for Tonjenae. She loved Ron, but it was obvious that no amount of love from nine women would make him stop loving his wife of over three decades.

Insensitive to Tonjenae's hurt, he asked, "You really think I have a chance to get my wife back?"

"Absolutely," she answered with a pained smile.

Ron then passionately kissed Tonjenae, which confused her. Next, he called the attorney to get three cars liquidated to pay off his debt to the company, as well as their fees.

He liked Tonjenae holding his hand through the process of his legal dealings involving his marriage, eviction, and business woes. He looked at her as his rock, which is why she got to sleep in his bed with him from then on. In his mind, she was Ava's replacement.

Two weeks later, they all moved into the house Tonjenae found; however, she let the women know that they'd have to figure out who would get to stay since some would have to leave before the babies began arriving. That angered the others. They wanted Ron to be with them and their babies, and to them, it seemed as if Tonjenae was setting the ball in motion to eliminate them all from Ron's life.

26

Winter was in full effect. Hormones were running rampant from nine women; medical costs were mounting; funds were running low; drama was never-ending; and for the first time ever, Ron's sex drive was almost non-existent…a recipe for more drama. Valentine's Day was the worst of all because some of the very pregnant girls threatened to jump Tonjenae if she dared to try to have him to herself on that day. That prompted Ron to liquidate yet another one of his cars, to find a second home nearby with five-bedrooms, as well. There he sent anyone who had a problem with his growing relationship with Tonjenae. That was Erica, Kennedy, Angela, Toni, and Sherrell. At her mother's insistence, Sherita volunteered to go to be near her sister. Shirleen, Tonjenae, and Kendra were the ones lucky enough to stay in the house with Ron, and for the most part, life had become much more peaceful. However, it disturbed Shirleen that he would go to the other house each day and, in her mind, take too long to return.

When Erica went into labor, Shirleen was sure to remind Ron that Erica's baby might belong to the bishop, the old store owner, or her mother's boyfriend. Still, Ron was present for the birth of his son…Ron Jr. In that moment, he didn't care about anything else other than finally having a son to carry on his name. He was so excited that he almost rebuked the notion of a paternity test. However, Kendra suggested that each of them get a paternity test done to remove any doubt. Most oddly, somehow Tonjenae's daughter was the first to be born…two weeks before Erica's son, although Erica was the first to claim being pregnant. Tonjenae named their daughter,

Rondenae, which was pleasing to Ron but not appreciated by Erica, who had already planned to name her son, Ronald Jr. Erica also didn't have any appreciation for Kendra naming her son, Rondell, which was a spin on Ron's name. Even Kendra went to Ron questioning why Tonjenae's child was born first if Erica claimed to be pregnant first. Having a son with his name, it didn't matter to him.

Most of the ladies were annoyed when the paternity test confirmed that Ron was indeed the father of Ron Jr. More disturbing, he moved Erica back into the house with him.

*****

"When are you going to pay these girls what you owe them?" Shirley Walker, the mother of Sherita, Shirleen and Sherrell, asked Ron when she went to see Shirleen and her baby who were staying in the house with Ron.

"I'm taking care of a lot of medical bills, food, diapers, and everything else. Back off!"

"You better be taking care of everything, but you also better make sure you pay these girls what you owe them. You're a dirty old man that ain't have no business taking advantage of these children."

"Didn't nobody take advantage of anybody," Kendra said, defending Ron.

"Be quiet and stay in a child's place, child. Stay out of grown folk conversation," Shirley chastised her.

"Bitch, I know you didn't just try to come for my motherfuckin' daughter, 'cause you know we can take this shit to the street, bitch!" Kendra's mother, Rochelle Thomas, said while taking off her earrings. "You wanna talk about somebody, when you ain't but fourteen or fifteen years older than your child. You better go find the man you was ho'ing around with back then and tell him that HE took advantage of a child."

"Don't try to act like you know me or anything about my

family. You need to concern yourself with the town slut, your daughter."

Rochelle stood at five-foot-three but charged at Shirley, who stood five inches taller. Ron was able to grab her.

"Oh no! You two will not be in my house fighting around my children. If you can't respect me, my children, and their mothers, stay the fuck out. You'll just have to wait until they choose to visit you," he yelled.

"I'm fine with staying away from this mess, but I still wanna know when you plan on paying my three daughters and my two nieces the five thousand dollars you promised to get them to go along with this bullshit. Your ass should be locked up, and believe me, I tried. I'll do anything to help my babies."

"Help them?" Ron asked, annoyed. "You had your children out there having sex with the preacher and a grocery store owner. How the fuck was that helping them? They were thirteen and fourteen years old, but you're standing in my house accusing me of doing something sinister. Even worse, you still sit up in that man's church every week and still want your daughters to give him whatever he wants so you can be alright. No! The reason your girls prefer to be here with me is because it's better than being pimped out by their own mother."

"That's a lie! That's a damn lie!" Shirley yelled with tears in her eyes.

"Momma, you forget I know the truth," Shirleen said, speaking up. "We all know the truth. That is not a lie."

"Shirleen, how could you say something like that about your momma?" Shirley cried.

"Aunt Shirley, please don't make me bring up about the first time you sent me to see Bishop and told me to do whatever he said," Tonjenae voiced as tears wet her face.

"This is all lies!" Shirley said again. "I have to get out of here. I can't believe you all are doing this to me, telling these lies." She grabbed her coat and ran to the door. "He's got you all brainwashed."

"Bye, bitch!" Rochelle yelled.

Ron hugged Shirleen and Tonjenae, who were both very emotional. Erica sat and watched with envy.

27

Tonjenae reluctantly left her baby at home with Kendra, Shirleen, and Erica so she could attend yet another court date with Ron, whereas he was being sued by his company for an outstanding balance that came in after his first legal battle with them.

"Mr. Johnson, you still owe over sixty-three thousand dollars to the company that you may have started, but no longer own and are no longer employed with. I understand you have previously paid back a debt in excess of three hundred thousand dollars, but only after being threatened with imprisonment. Four months have gone by since the request for this latest payment. Yet, you haven't paid a nickel on this sixty-three-thousand-dollar debt. Do you think it's just going to go away? Did any of the other employees benefit from the sixty-three thousand you spent?" the judge asked.

"Sir, my client just had children born, and right now, the money he has is tied up into caring for those children. In no way is it his intention to ignore this debt, and if possible, he'd like to try to work out some type of arrangement. As you already stated, his company–where he had been employed for over thirty-five years–chose to terminate his employment and CEO position, thereby making it virtually impossible to work off his debt," Ron's attorney stated.

"How old are you, Mr. Johnson?"

"My client is sixty-two years old."

"And you said he just had children…plural? Were they twins?"

The attorney cringed, not wanting to have to answer that

question but knowing he had no other choice. "Unfortunately, my client was going through a very rough emotional period on the heels of his divorce and ultimately exercised poor judgment, impregnating multiple women in a short time span."

"Multiple women? How many is multiple? Is this how the debt came about, impregnating multiple women?"

The attorney closed his eyes and took a deep breath before mumbling, "Nine."

"Nine?! Nine women have birthed him nine children, and he's too broke to care for them, which means we, the taxpayers, will have to pay for his poor judgment?"

The attorney had no answer.

"So, what is he doing for income?"

"My client only received a very small payment from his wife after the divorce, and he has pretty much liquidated most of his assets to pay off his debt. He was also forced to defend himself in a frivolous lawsuit in another court by a man who brutally assaulted and robbed my client, causing him to have to shell out even more in legal fees. That case was ultimately thrown out, but it made its way before a judge, forcing us to go to court."

"Is your firm taking this case pro bono, or is Mr. Johnson's legal debt continuing to mount?"

"Our firm is not on a pro bono basis at this time. We are, however, willing to try to work out an arrangement on this case since it does stem from the previous case with this same plaintiff."

"Seems like your client might wanna hurry up and get that resume together so he can find himself a job. Nine babies, ongoing legal issues, and a sixty-three-thousand-dollar debt. He needs a job. I don't know why he doesn't already have one. Why *doesn't* he have a job?"

"Your Honor, my client is sixty-two years old."

"And I'm seventy. What's your point? Go tell someone who might have some sympathy. I don't care if he has to clean floors in McDonald's or greet customers in Walmart. He's going to pay his debt and make sure those children are taken care of, 'cause if I get wind that just one of them babies are being cared for with taxpayer dollars, I'll personally find a way for Mr. Johnson to be locked up. But, that's a different case for a different court. With regards to this case set before me, I'm giving Mr. Johnson thirty days to find a way to get his debt paid, or I will send this case over to criminal court and allow him to be prosecuted. I'm not sure if your client thinks it's a game to take food from his employees' mouths, but I'm not going to let that happen. They were generous in bringing this to civil court instead of criminal court, and now your client will settle this. If it's not satisfied, I will send it for criminal prosecution."

"Your Honor, where is my client going to raise that kind of money within thirty days?"

"You're asking me as if I care," the judge callously responded.

"Your Honor, if you don't mind, I have something to add to this case." Ariana stood up from the back of the court, where she was previously unseen, and walked to the plaintiff's table.

Everyone turned in surprise.

"And you are?" the judge asked.

"My name is Ariana Johnson. I used to be the defendant's youngest daughter, before he brought his circus to town," she said, making a sour face and rolling her eyes at Ron.

"Interesting. You went to the plaintiff's table and not the defendant's table," he commented, amused.

"Yes, Your Honor. Although I'm here to offer the defendant a way to avoid prison, I in no way condone any of his activities, particularly at the expense of my mother, myself, or my siblings."

"Well, I'm definitely interested in hearing your offer." the judge said as he smiled at Ariana, sensing her pain caused by her father.

"If my father is willing to relinquish his remaining shares in our company and forego any future dividends, we will erase the debt."

"But that's my source of income," Ron yelled.

"Then go to prison for the rest of your life and see how that works out for you," Ariana yelled back, fighting tears.

"That sounds like a very generous offer. I highly suggest you discuss it with your client before I write up the order of this court, which would include a move to criminal court in thirty days," the judge said, addressing Ron's attorney.

Ron placed his forehead on the desk. Feeling defeated, he just wanted his life to be over right then. The attorney put his hand on Ron's back and whispered to him. With his head still down, Ron mumbled a response.

The attorney stood back up and said, "Your Honor, my client accepts Miss Johnson's generous offer."

Ariana blew out the deep breath she'd been holding in, and the tears fell from her eyes. She bent to speak with their attorneys, then turned and left the courtroom. After she exited, the judge scolded Ron some more with regards to the nine babies and the damage he had caused his preexisting children.

Like a trooper, Tonjenae provided comforting arms to a broken Ron as they left the courtroom. Little did she know, she would be met with her own conflict upon entering their home.

The girls were crying, and Shirleen was holding Tonjenae's daughter for dear life while continually kissing her.

"What the hell is going on?" Ron asked.

Sensing something was wrong, Tonjenae ran to take her baby from her cousin.

"I swear it was an accident," Erica volunteered.

"It was not a fucking accident! She did that shit on purpose," Kendra yelled. "Hating-ass bitch been complaining about Tonjenae always with Ron and acting like nobody else's baby matters. She went and picked up the baby, then just let her go. She dropped the baby on the floor. That's so fucked up! The baby was sleep. She wasn't crying. There was no need for Erica to touch the baby."

Kendra was so angry that she was foaming at the mouth as

the tears poured down her face.

Ron grabbed the baby from Tonjenae to examine her. Tonjenae rushed over and punched Erica, and the pair started fighting. Shirleen jumped in to beat Erica.

Convinced that the baby seemed fine, Ron carefully laid her down and hurried to break up the fight. He ordered Erica to leave his son and go stay at the other house. She begged and pleaded, but he was done with her. Once Erica was out of the house, he packed his son, Tonjenae, and their daughter into the car to take the baby to the hospital to get checked out. Fortunately, all was well with the baby.

28

Things were getting tighter with money, and medical bills were coming from every direction. He was not able to pay any of the women the other half of the ten thousand dollars he promised. Ron had been sending out resumes but receiving no promising callbacks for a job. The ones that did call back only seemed to want to know why he would step down from a well-paying position at his own company to work at someone else's company for a fraction of the salary. Things became so tight that the ladies each had to go out and find jobs. Most of them were glad about getting a job and putting their monies together to help Ron get back on his feet. Erica even suggested helping him start up a new company that eventually all of them could run. Nonetheless, they knew they had to find a way to get some income.

Erica and Kennedy decided to go to Ron's family company, Johnson, Inc., to apply for any position they could get. They didn't let Ron, Kendra, Tonjenae, or Shirleen know, and since Ariana and Ava were hardly there, they didn't see the girls working there. A few days later, Angela and Toni also went for a job. Ron didn't have a clue where they were working. Through Erica's due diligence, Sherrell learned that there was a job opening at Rashaun's main office, and she went to get that job. Sherita had already begun working at a bank. Tonjenae was able to get a job at the hospital, while Kendra took a job at a hotel. Shirleen reenrolled in school, taking online classes, and helped to care for the babies.

Erica devised a plan to steal blank checks, fill them out, and deposit them into the bank account that Sherita had opened and added Ron's name to.

"What if we get caught and they're able to tell where the checks came from?" Angela asked, not wanting to be a part of the plan.

"They have no way of knowing anything. I saw where they keep the thing to stamp signatures on the checks. When Toni's cleaning that floor at night, she can just use the stamp to endorse a bunch of checks, and we can add an amount," Erica masterminded.

"Remember, they tried to put Ron in prison when they found out he was stealing from the company," Kennedy reminded them.

"That's because Ron was stupid, greedy, and reckless, and he was spending a lot of money every day. All we need is to get enough to be able to open up an office somewhere and start a business. Not only that, but don't you think our children should be taken care of and living well like his other kids?" Erica asked. "Our children deserve the same as the others have."

"I agree," Sherrell said. "His son, Rashaun, has a fancy office, and the staff be having fancy lunches all the time. We should be able to have that, and once we get our company going, we will have all of that and then some."

"We still haven't decided on what kind of company we're going to have," Sherita said.

"We'll figure it out once we get an office, but first, we have to get this money," Erica told them. "Sherrell, you think you can get some money from where you're working?"

"I saw where they keep this big envelope with cash in it. It looks like a lot of big bills. I'm sure I can take some without them even knowing."

"Me and Erica used to take money out the drawer all the time when we had that one job at the store," Toni bragged.

"Half the time I wouldn't ring stuff up. I'd tell the customer any ol' price, and when they left, I'd take that money out of the drawer and pocket it. Shoot, that damn store wasn't paying shit, and I had to pay my rent," Erica stated, then laughed.

"I used to steal money from the diner all the time. They never knew," Sherrell also bragged.

"I know one thing, y'all better not let them bitches at the other house find out. You know they'll run their mouths and tell Ron. Then he'll act all stupid," Erica said, annoyed particularly by the thought of Tonjenae.

"You right," Sherita said. "I can't believe he won't let you see your own son every day. I used to think he was really in love with you, but now everything is about Tonjenae."

"Well, hopefully when everything comes together, he'll love me again. I mean, I know he loves me. He's just mad at me right now. I don't blame him, though." Erica pretended to be stoic, but inside, she was fuming as well as hurt.

"Come on, y'all. Let's make a pact. We're all in this together for our children. No turning back," Kennedy said, holding her hand outstretched with the palm down so Erica, Sherrell, Sherita, Angela, and Toni could pile their hand on top of each other's. They did and then went forth with their plan.

29

"Hey, Erica, there's someone here to see you in the conference room."

Erica looked confused, then thought maybe it was her mother.

"Thanks, Misty," Erica told her co-worker.

When Erica arrived at the conference room, Ava, Ariana, a gentleman from finance, the lady from HR, as well as two other middle-aged men who she had never seen before were waiting inside. Her first mind was to run, but then she figured Ava and Ariana had finally discovered that one of Ron's women were working in their company, but that thought only made Erica wonder why Kennedy wasn't in the room, too.

Maybe they haven't recognized Kennedy from being at the house when they came that time when Ron was in the hospital, she thought.

One of the middle-aged men stood by the door while the others sat in one of the smaller conference rooms. There wasn't a seat for Erica to sit, which she felt was rude of them. So, she had to stand. It felt as if she were standing before a firing squad.

"Hi, Erica. I don't think we've been formerly introduced," Ava started, surprisingly pleasant. "In case you've forgotten, I'm Ava Johnson and this is my daughter, Ariana Johnson. I am the principal owner of this company that I share with my children along with our dedicated employees. Here, we like to keep our eyes on our employees so they may be properly rewarded with what they deserve. That's how we know to promote employees or fully utilize their skills in better ways that will help this company to continually grow. Having dedicated employees who provide outstanding performance has helped this company have annual earnings in excess of seventy-five million dollars, and it allows us to provide many jobs as well as give back to the community. I know you haven't been in the Metro Atlanta area too long, but we are very active in the community and have many friends everywhere. For example, here's two of our very good friends from the Forensic Crimes Division of the FBI," she said, pointing to the two unknown faces.

"When you came to work here three weeks ago, I knew who you were," she continued. "I knew you were one of several of my former husband's whores that he impregnated, but I allowed you to stay here because I'm not as cruel as some would like to make me out to be. I knew of his current financial dilemma, as well as his struggling to care of nine babies. I don't think it's at all fair what you or he have done, bringing a baby into this world as part of a revenge plot. Nonetheless, the baby…or should I say babies…should not have to suffer. As such, I graciously allowed you to be employed here, even though you possess no real skills. Your friends, as well. I figured I'd allow you to do what you had to do to make sure your child is taken care of since I know he can't provide. And just like all of our employees who we keep our eyes on, we watched you, too.

"You do recognize Laura from HR, who keeps me informed of everything, and there's Daniel from finance? Well, Laura let me know the minute you and the other young ladies came here for a job, and I gave her the green light to hire you all, with explicit instructions to keep an eye on each of you. And when Dan came to me about severe financial abnormalities occurring only a week after your arrival, it didn't take a rocket scientist to track the issues, thanks to us living in the wonderful age of technology. Now, I'm not sure if the other whore–who was caught having sex with my husband–made you aware that this entire building is wired with video and audio cameras. That was my darling daughter's idea after some jackass started stealing the office supplies. Sadly, he, too, was a new hire."

Erica could feel her heart racing and her breaths getting shorter. She wondered if the others could hear the booming heartbeat that she was hearing in her head. Her eyes scanned the room for an escape, but she already knew she was an animal being prepared for the slaughter.

"I'm not sure if you have any clue how smart my children are," Ava continued. Funny thing, when people are dumb, they tend to think everyone is as dumb as they are. Your friend, Sherrell… Now that is one dumb broad. But, I think her sister, Sherita, takes the cake. Let me help you understand how the finance department works. Their job is to keep count of the money, including what is earned and what is spent. And when something doesn't balance out, we have special people like Dan to figure out where things went wrong. We then communicate those things to our special friends over at the FBI, and ultimately, they come to lock up the special people, who obviously spent a lifetime riding the short, yellow bus. No disrespect to real handicap people. But, you, Erica…you are a special brand of stupid. You and your silly whore friends who will now spend the next twenty years in prison while your babies end up wherever and with whoever since Ron is now broke as hell."

Ava nodded to the man standing, and he approached Erica as the other middle-aged gentleman stood up.

"Erica Dinkins, you are under arrest. You have the right to remain silent…"

"Wait!" Erica yelled. "We were only doing what Ron told us to do. He's the one who told us to get jobs here and take money from here so he could build a new company and be able to take care of our children the way your children are taken care of," she cried out in desperation.

"Hold up!" Ariana laughed. "So now you're trying to tell me that my father is such a stupid businessman that he wouldn't know that check-stealing scheme wouldn't work out for him, especially after having just finished a lengthy legal battle for embezzlement?"

"I hate to say it, but I think he really is that stupid," Daniel admitted. "Look how many checks he wrote out to Cash in addition to the purchases he made using the company credit cards."

"Yeah, but at least he was still an employee and held shares in the company. He wouldn't turn right around and put himself in the exact same position after escaping going to prison only a couple of months ago."

"The funds were deposited into a bank account with his name on it," Daniel continued, debating with Ariana.

"Then they'll all go to prison as far as I'm concerned," Ava said. "Get that bitch out of my building, then go 'round up the rest of them."

As Erica was being carried out in handcuffs, she screamed as if someone were killing her.

By that night, Erica, Kennedy, Angela, Toni, Sherrell, Sherita, *and* Ron were all in federal custody.

30

Ron sat in the interrogation room being grilled on his involvement with the embezzlement scheme Erica put together.

"This is absolutely ridiculous. I didn't even know the girls were working at my company. I would have never told them to go there to work. That's insane. I also didn't know anything about this bank account with my name on it. I would have had to sign for it, and I didn't. I know enough about business and banking to know stuff is traceable."

"If you're so smart, why did you just finish settling an almost four-hundred-thousand-dollar embezzlement debt?" the agent asked.

"It was my company. I created it and ran it for thirty-five years. I didn't know spending the money I earned my company was a crime. Had I known, I would not have done it. However, having learned that lesson, it would be pure insanity for me to turn right around and orchestrate some foolish plan such as that."

"What about this new company you are forming?"

Ron looked confused. "Company? What new company?"

"The ladies said you had them stealing the money so you can start a new company."

"I am sixty-two-damn-years-old. Do you really think I have any interest in starting a new company? I have babies to look after while their mothers are at work. When am I supposed to have time to build and run a new company?"

"Why would the ladies say you put them up to it?"

"First, I can't imagine them actually telling you some

nonsense like that. However, if anyone said that, it would be Erica, who I know is angry with me because I won't allow her to be alone with our son. Erica tried to cause harm to one of my other babies out of jealousy. So, I told her that she could no longer live in the same house as my daughter who she tried to harm and me."

"Okay, that explains Erica, but why would the others also say it?"

"The only ones who would say that are the ladies that live in my second house. They have this jealousy thing going on. The reason they are in that second house is because they were all trying to fight the one who I am the closest to. I can bet my life on the fact that the ones who live in the house with me have no knowledge of this so-called new company or the place those girls were working. They don't even get along."

"Did you know Sherita Walker was working at a bank?"

"That I did know. However, she was supposedly still in training. So, I'm not sure how she was able to make those bank deposits. I didn't even know she was placed in a branch already. She told me something about having six weeks of classroom training."

"No, she's been in the branch for three weeks now and has been depositing checks each day. The good thing is, none of the deposited funds have been withdrawn, but the cash stolen was pocketed."

Ron covered his face. "I don't know what in the hell would make them do something so fucking stupid. They have babies. *We* have babies. Why would they want to risk me being imprisoned behind their mess? And I wouldn't imagine them being stupid enough to set themselves up to be imprisoned. What I find even more disturbing is, why would they choose my family's businesses to go and try to steal from?"

"Miss Dinkins said you told them to go there because you knew your way around and you had taken her there a time or two before when you lost your keys."

"Erica is lying to you!" Ron yelled. "Yes, I took her to my

office before when I was still working there. No, I would never put her–or any of them–in a position to have to do battle with my wife. I know my wife knows what they look like, so that would be crazy of me because I know Ava would crush them. So, again, I would never have sent either of them to work there. If I sent them, why wouldn't I have sent the ones living in the house with me, as well?"

A second agent came in and called for the first one to step outside the room.

When the first agent returned, he said, "You may have some allies after all."

"Huh?" Ron asked, puzzled.

"Angela Williams. She decided to break from the others, saying Erica was the mastermind behind the whole plan and you didn't know anything about them working at your wife and son's company. She said she was happy to have found a good job and didn't want to go along with Erica's plan. She said they didn't want you to know they worked there or anything about the plan to steal because you would've gotten angry with them for bothering your wife, who you're still stuck on. The crazy thing is, Angela never worked on the floor where the other girl–Toni, I believe–was stamping the checks that Kennedy was stealing. Other than Erica now being accused of being the mastermind behind this plot to either destroy you or help you get on your feet, her hands are clean. She was seen getting in the car with Kennedy on a couple of occasions, but that's all we have on Erica."

"But you just said Angela told you?" Ron stated as a question.

"The five others say differently. They all point the finger at you. So, where things stand at this moment, you, Sherita, Kennedy, Toni, and Sherrell will be taken into custody. As for Erica, I'm not sure we can make a case against her without the others, and right now, they seem to hate you a whole lot more than they hate her…or maybe they're simply telling the truth. Angela may get cut loose since she really doesn't seem to be involved, other than possibly having knowledge of their plan. Maybe we'll find another charge for her."

"You're keeping me?! What?! Why?! I had no knowledge of any of this. I just started a new job yesterday that allows me to work from home and watch my children. The pay isn't what I'm used to, but it's enough for me to take care of my kids and keep them out of the welfare system. If you lock me up now, based on the silly accusations of some bitter young girls, I'll lose the job and won't be able to provide for my family when I am exonerated. Then a judge will be trying to lock me up for being a deadbeat dad."

"I'm sorry, but these are the women you picked. Perhaps you should've tried sticking with one woman rather than creating a pack of bitter, scorned women," the agent said before exiting the interrogation room.

31

Ron returned home three days later after being held in custody and waiting to see a judge who allowed him to be released on his own recognizant since he felt the case against Ron was very weak.

He returned home just in time to see Tonjenae tearfully packing to leave.

"Tonji, where are you going? Where are the other babies?" he asked.

"They're gone. They left. Erica came and took her son, threatening to call the police on me. Aunt Shirley came to get Shirleen along with Toni, Sherita, and Sherrell's babies. She told me to come, too, but I was hoping you'd come back and then we could be a happy family."

"Great! We will be. Everything's going to be perfect. You'll see. I love you so much," he said, cradling her face before kissing her lips.

"I love you, too, Ron, but I can't stay with you. You say you love me, but you're still in love with your wife. No matter what I say or do, you find a way to compare me to her. You haven't really said anything bad, but it hurts me every time you do it. You tell me I'm good at handling the finances like Ava. You tell me I cook almost as good as Ava. You tell me that I'm smart like Ava and a good mother like Ava. Never have you given me credit for just being me. I'm now twenty-two years old, and I'm thinking if I get on with my life right now, I can get myself together and maybe one day have a family of my own with a man who will love and adore me for being me, and not constantly compare me to his previous wife. I am so in love with the daughter that we made together, and I'll be forever grateful for her. Not a single regret about how she was made. Regardless, it's time for me to go on with my life."

"You're just going to take our daughter away from me? I've lost everything for all of you, and now you're taking the last thing I have left?"

"I have another aunt up near Washington, D.C. She told me that I could come there and maybe find a good government job so I can provide for our daughter. I would never deny you seeing our daughter, but there's nothing but a bunch of pain here for me. I love you and probably always will, but you love your wife and always will. No woman will ever be able to compete with what you had with your wife. She loved you through almost thirty years of cheating on her. I couldn't even love you that much.

"I also look at how you treated your older kids and wondered why all of them hate you so much. Now I can't help but wonder will you be just as mean to our daughter. Will you go around telling people our child is not your child like you did with your son, Rashaun? That's got to be the most hurtful feeling ever. During these past three days while you were locked up, I thought if you were a good father and had a good relationship with Rashaun, there is no way Sherrell would have been able to go to work at his company without you knowing about it immediately. The same with the others. You would have been kept in the loop about Erica and the others going there for a job. Even worse, I asked you many times to pick up the phone and call your children or even thank your daughter for saving your ass when you went to court. But, you'd refuse and blame everyone but yourself.

"And while you like to compare me to your wife, I have to say I can't blame her for doing what she had to do to save herself, her children, and the company. What do you have to show for all the money you wasted on women and a lot of empty sex? You're up there in age; you're sixty-two years old. You're still suffering from those injuries from a while back when you were in the hospital, and all because the nine women you had still wasn't enough for you. So, you went out and sexed another, which ended up in you getting beaten and robbed. I realize now you're not the kind of man I deserve in my life. I have a daughter to think about now, and she deserves better than the way you will treat me or her. I definitely can't allow my daughter to be further exposed to Erica, because she'll forever be around with the child the two of you share. I was actually terrified when she came for her son because she's evil. You like to call her eyes mesmerizing or hypnotizing; they're evil. I see the devil every time I look at her eyes.

"But, another big reason I have to go I because I love you too much to cheat on you. I'm not interested in being in sexual relationships with girls. I did that for you, even though I didn't enjoy it, and I'll have to live with the shame of what I've done. I'm twenty-two, and I have needs. You've been under so much stress lately that you don't even work down there anymore. Kendra said it was because you're old. I hate to say it, but Bishop Rogers is older than you and his still works. And I don't want to be sitting around like your wife did for thirty years, while you do nothing but be with other women and then try to give me all your money for me to just shut up and be a good wife. I know I deserve better than that. Even your wife told us that long ago when she came to the house…we deserve better."

Ron sat on the sofa bent over with his face in his hands. He couldn't argue with anything Tonjenae said. He wanted to tell her that she was just as long-winded and gave sensible speeches *just like his wife*, but thought against it, as that would only be another slap in the face to Tonjenae.

When he didn't know what else to say, he asked, "Could you at least stay with me tonight so we can spend time together with our daughter one last time as a family?"

It was as if someone had punched Tonjenae in the midsection, knocking the wind out of her. She fell to the floor and cried while constantly repeating, "Yes! Yes! Yes! Yes!"

The rest of the day was perfect. The love they made that

night was like no other, giving Ron hope that Tonjenae might change her mind and stay. However, first thing the next morning, Tonjenae loaded her car with her minimal possessions, her baby, and herself, leaving a distraught Ron in her rearview mirror.

32

"Thank you for agreeing to meet with me. It would have been fine for you to come by the house. I'm there alone now. Everyone has left me."

"Oh, no. There's no way I'm stepping foot back into your dens of inequity." Ava chuckled. "Besides, I figured you could use this lobster and champagne lunch treat since I'm sure it's been a while for you."

Ron graciously smiled through his pain.

"What happened to that one girl? Can't remember her name. I thought she'd stick with you 'til death. I actually kind of had a grain of respect for that one, unlike the others."

"Tonjenae?" Ron asked.

"Don't get me to lying. I honestly wouldn't know one name from the other. I know Ariana told me that she was with you in court a while back. I also heard she tried to tell the federal agents that none of you had any knowledge about that new shit. If Miss Erica thinks she's gotten away with it, she is sadly mistaken."

"She tried to kill my daughter. Tonjenae's child."

Ava's eyes widened. "Are you fucking serious?"

"That day when Tonjenae was with me in court, Erica picked up the baby and dropped her to the ground, claiming it was an accident. The others said it was no accident and that the baby was asleep when Erica decided to pick her up. They didn't know what to do. I took the baby to the hospital and everything checked out, but I made Erica leave and go stay with the others. I wouldn't even let her take my son with her. After that, she couldn't come around my son unless I was there to watch her and only if I said so."

Each time Ron would talk about his other children to Ava as if she was his good friend instead of the woman who sat foolishly for thirty years waiting for him to change his philandering ways, she would experience fluttering and feel like daggers were poking in her chest. Still, she behaved as a friend.

"Well, I guess that would explain why she was out to get you. Why did the others turn on you?" she asked.

Deeply troubled, Ron closed his eyes. "I really don't know. It was Tonjenae who told me about how manipulative Erica is, but I didn't want to believe it, even when Erica practically admitted it herself. Talk about feeling like an old fool. Speaking of which, I know you're probably sick of hearing my apologies, but, Ava, I am so very sorry for all the pain, grief, years of sorrow, and neglect I caused you and our five children. I'm especially sorry for doubting my beautiful, precious son that you gave me. I'm sorry I wasn't more involved in our children's lives and for not taking you and our children on shitloads of vacations. I'm sorry for bleeding our family financially, emotionally, psychologically, and every other way. I'm sorry I treated you, the mother of our children, with pure disrespect for thirty years, while I set out to make you look like a fool to anyone who was on the outside looking in. The crazy thing is, the young girl, who I thought could maybe somehow fill your shoes, was the one to tell me how foolish I was to treat you and our children the way I did."

Although Ava's eyes began watering, she laughed. "Oh, that must have been that one girl I said had a half of grain of sense."

Ron smiled. "Yes, that was Tonjenae. She told me that I frequently compared her to you, and she felt like with you is where I belong. She left me with a lot to think about, but the main thing I thought is that I really owe you and our children an apology. I know I've apologized a million times or more, but this is the first time I've had the opportunity to see things from the outside and been able to take a look at how stupid I have been for so long. I want to see how we can mend our relationship…our family."

Ava's poker smile didn't give him any clue as to how she felt about fixing their family.

After an awkward silence, he asked, "I've talked so much about my issues that I don't even know what's going on in your lives. How are the kids? Where are they?"

Ava chuckled, relieved that he finally inquired about them.

"Everyone's well. Ariana got a part in a movie. Can you believe that? Our daughter, the big time Hollywood star. Even though it's a small role, it's a start to what she wants to do with her life. Shara's been in Africa for a few months now. She's planning on spending time in all the countries of the world, so she'll be in Africa for a while."

"Oh no! Africa? How long will she be gone?" Ron was saddened. "How will I get a chance to try to mend our relationship?"

"Try going to visit her there, just you and she, and hash out all of your differences. Apologize."

Ron frowned. "Yeah, that would have been wonderful, but I can't leave the state with this latest pending criminal case. They took my passport, and I had just enough money to pay for a round-trip bus fare to get here."

Ava felt like she had been punched in the gut. It hurt her to know the man she would love forever was so down…even if he did deserve it.

"How are you eating and paying your bills?" she asked, genuinely concerned.

He was almost too embarrassed to answer.

"Truth is, I have an eviction notice, shut-off notice for the lights, and been eating those packs of noodles. So, I'm especially thankful for this lobster lunch." He chuckled through his pain and shame.

"Ron, I need you to know, yes, I did do things to hurt you. You told me I was going to have to share you, but I thought those were empty threats, although I had pretty much already been sharing you our entire marriage. Never would I have thought you'd do something like that to me. I couldn't even imagine you suggesting something so insane to me after you had already given me those divorce papers that would leave you with absolutely nothing. Then you brought that girl into our home, I knew then that nothing could ever cut me deeper or hurt me more. I didn't know if you were having some mental issues, if you really did want me to divorce you, or if you were just being selfish and didn't give a fuck how anything affected me. You can't begin to imagine the devastation I felt when I saw you bring that girl into our home, into our marital bed, and you did it only because you wanted to punish me for only God knows what.

"So, yes, I've done things to destroy you, beginning with putting poison ivy in the bed and making you think you had shingles. I was the one who made sure they kept you locked up in the hospital on an involuntary psychiatric hold after that silly little girl bragged to Guida about how you were planning to impregnate nine girls and give them ten thousand dollars each, as well as move them into our home. Surely that was evidence that you were going insane. There was no way I could simply sit back and allow that. I was hoping after fifteen days of isolation, you'd come to your senses, but you didn't. Instead, you got worse. You decided to rob the company for damn near half a million dollars in just a matter of a few short months, all to wine and dine that pack of whores. And damn right I had every fixture removed from the home so they couldn't enjoy it, but I never thought you'd be dumb enough to use company funds to replace everything for those bimbos. I knew you had enough cash in your safe to get you through. After the level of persistence that you showed to try to hurt me, I figured I'd just sit back and watch you hang yourself."

"Hangman!" Ron laughed deliriously.

Ava looked confused. "Is that supposed to mean something?"

"You wouldn't even believe it if I told you."

"Try me. I didn't believe a lot of stuff before now."

"Last year, I saw a psychic lady. I was just passing through, and someone directed me to her. The first words from her mouth were 'man-whore'!"

Ava cracked up laughing. "Wow!"

"Yeah, so naturally, I was intrigued. She told me about how stupid I was and that I destroyed my marriage. She had me pull three cards. First card was death. I thought I was going to die. I thought you and the kids were plotting to kill me. Next card was the fool, and the last card was the hangman. She told me that things would get so bad that I'd be wishing for death because of all the foolish things I was doing."

"Wow!" Ava said again. "You need to keep in touch with her so you can know which steps to take in your life to keep from doing foolish things."

It was Ron's turn to laugh. "I asked, but she told me that I can never come see her again because my negative energy drained and stressed her."

Ava frowned. "Damn! That's bad. Usually those people want to take your money."

Ron was happy that he and Ava were in a good place and laughing.

"Ava, I know I've done a lot of damage and we have a long way to go before our relationship is fixed, but I'd like to come home. I can stay in a different room if you'd like. I won't try to pressure you. Maybe one day after all my legal woes are behind me, we can take those overdue vacations together."

Ava smiled warmly. "Ron, I don't live in Georgia anymore. I found a cute little condo just for me in Miami, and before you ask…no, there is not—nor was there ever—any other man in my life. I gave the house to Rashaun, and now he uses it for business events. He still stays in his condo when he's in Atlanta. He has no desire to live in that house either. We were going to sell it, but he's been making a lot of money from it. Eve bought a condo in my building for when she comes to

Miami with her friends. She sold her condo here in Georgia. She's back primarily living in Jersey."

"Do you think I could come and see you in Miami once I'm cleared of everything?"

"Let me ask you this. How do you plan to support those nine babies? Four of the girls are locked up right now, and I'm assuming their families are caring for the children. That other girl is definitely going to be joining them. Do you plan on just ignoring those children as you did Shara before we were married, or are you finally going to step up and learn to be a father? You have a second chance to get this right, and I think those children need to be your priority right now. What's going to happen to your daughters? Will they fall prey to horny old men such as yourself? Your sons…what guidance and support will they have? Are they going to be gangbanging, drug dealing, robbing, and stealing like their silly-ass mothers?

"And how do you intend to pay nine child support orders? Because you know those kids are going into the welfare system, and a judge will be itching to lock your old, black ass up just for the free labor to the state."

Ron covered his face with his hands in shame.

"I don't know. When that psychic said I'd be praying for death, that was no lie or gimmick. I hate the hell that I have created for myself, my family, and those babies. Ava, I don't know what to do. I first felt my world crumbling when you left because you were my glue. I hadn't even realized how much you kept us together. I guess that's why I was always comparing Tonjenae to you, because she's so much like you in that manner. She would just take charge. But, now you're gone, she's gone, and I'm lost. Maybe I deserve to be locked up. That's the only time I'm not a danger to others."

"But, that doesn't help those babies in any way. I can't be back with you, and I'm not helping you raise those babies. However, I will handle your legal fees along with covering your rent and utilities for one year. I'm not putting a dime in your hand, though. Also, I will help you get a job, but you will not be earning more than seventy-five thousand dollars a year."

"Seventy-five thousand dollars?! How can I live on that? Child support's going to eat up all of that," Ron foolishly protested.

"Well, if you have a better offer, take that instead," she responded, annoyed with his ungrateful attitude.

"I'm sorry. I'm sorry. I should be saying thank you. Thank you so much."

"I'll also throw in a minivan and you can get medical insurance for the kids, not their mothers. I highly suggest you get custody of your children from those family members. Be sure to frequently see the ones you don't get full custody of, and that's that. Oh, and I'll see to it that the job will allow you to work from home as well as give you bonus earning potential. That's the best I can do for you, Ron. I don't owe you anything, but I'm doing this for those innocent babies who didn't do anything wrong. They're going to grow up all confused as sisters and brothers and cousins. That's crazy. So, yeah, this is for the children. You already hung yourself." She chuckled.

Ron deeply exhaled, his eyes filled with tears. "Thank you, Ava. I love you so much, and I really did fuck up a great thing losing you."

"Yes, you did. Yes, you did."

33

While at the park with five of his babies—including his son who he got back when Erica was locked up after the others finally came clean, exonerating Ron completely—he saw a familiar looking woman pushing a stroller and having what looked to be a stressful conversation on the phone.

"Chloe?" he said, recognizing her.

Terror caused her to drop her phone. She thought Ron was going to hurt her.

"I swear I had nothing to do with what my ex-husband did. I didn't know he was in town."

He chuckled and replied, "Calm down. I'm not angry. I probably deserved it. How are you? I see congratulations are in order. She's beautiful. How old is she? She looks almost the age of these little ones."

Chloe's eyes filled with tears. "She's your daughter. My ex-husband is not her father. I didn't know where you were or how to reach you. Truth is, I was terrified to see you because I heard they thought I set you up, but I swear I would never do something so stupid. Then I lost my job at the hospital behind his mess."

Ron covered his mouth. His eyes also filled with tears. He was both shocked and happy.

"So where are you staying these days?" he asked.

A single teardrop fell from her eye. "In a shelter. Family ain't worth a damn these days. Me and my baby have been in a shelter for like three months. I'm hoping to try to get into government housing so I can get back on my feet and hopefully get my nursing license reinstated. Then I can get a real job instead of working that Circle-K job I got to help feed us."

"Oh wow! I'm so sorry for messing up your life like that," he said, feeling horrible.

"I messed my own life up when I married that fool. He's moved on and living with some new girl. Let him be her problem. He should have been in jail for what he did to you."

In Ron's mind, he completely agreed but remembered the police saying something about they couldn't determine who was the primary aggressor, as well as questioning why Ron was in the hotel having sex with the man's wife.

The wheels turned in his mind as he considered her current predicament.

"Hey, I have custody of these five little ones, and I have four others that visit. Do you think you'd like to stay with us? I mean, it would be great to get to know this beautiful little girl. And with you being a nurse, that would be even better because I'm sure you'd be good with kids. It doesn't have to be any strings attached."

"Are you serious?" Chloe asked.

Ron wasn't sure if she was offended or delighted.

"Oh my God! I can't believe this! This has got to be the happiest day of my life!" she yelled.

She wanted to hug him, but he had a baby strapped to his front and back.

"Do you have a car still? If so, we can swing by the shelter, get your belongings, and then head to the house. It's in Mableton. I'm renting a five-bedroom."

"Everything I have is pretty much packed in my car. I don't leave anything in that shelter because it'll get stolen."

"Well then, let's pack the babies up and go home."

~The End~

Thank you for reading 9INE OF FOOLS. Now that you're all done, be sure to leave a review and let others know how much you've enjoyed the story. No spoiler alerts. If you have enjoyed this book, be sure to check out other books by The Queen that are currently available:

Tapioca Pudding Next Door
Trapped in the Closet
A Scorned Woman
Superwoman

The Between Sisters series, to include*:*
Between Sisters
Between More Sisters
Caught Up Between Sisters
The Evolution Between Sisters
Revenge Between Sisters
Sister's Daughter
Never Again Between Sisters

As a bonus, also included is a short sample of another new release, **Butterscotch Pudding Next Door**, which is a combined follow up of **Tapioca Pudding Next Door** and **Never Again Between Sisters**.

To stay informed about what other books **Queendom Dreams Publishing** will be releasing, please visit: www.queendomdreamspublishing.com.

About The Queen

The Queen has been writing for many years, ranging in short stories, poetry, plays, professional and other writings. She is a native of (Queensbridge) Long Island City, New York. Her debut novel was Between Sisters (of the Between Sisters' series). Her education includes Business and International Business Administration, as well as Travel & Tourism. When she's not writing, she loves to travel to sunny climates with clear and turquoise waters or near mountains for inspiration.

Butterscotch Pudding Next Door

By The Queen

1

"Butterscotch Pudding, here to see my sister, Chocolate Pudding"

"Huh?! What?!" the prison guard asked.

"I'd like to see my sister. Her name is Chocolate Pudding. I think she was just transferred to this prison about a month ago. My name is Butterscotch Pudding."

The guard unsuccessfully maintained a hard, stoned-face, when she burst out into laughter. "Alrighty! Your momma actually named you that?"

Butterscotch wasn't the least bit amused. She had already endured a rough life because of the silly name bestowed upon her at birth. She couldn't understand what would possess anyone to name their children after different flavors of puddings, but that's the names she and her sisters, Chocolate, Tapioca and Vanilla, received at birth from their mother, Portia Pudding. "Unfortunately, we don't get to all pick our own names at birth," Butterscotch sarcastically responded.

The guard immediately straightened up, not appreciative of the tone Butterscotch was giving her. "Well, I'm looking in the computer here and I don't see you on the list of visitors, and beside that, your sister is not allowed visitors at this time. Perhaps you might want to write her a letter, asking her to add you to her list of visitors for when she is able to have them."

"I'm her sister, for crying out loud. Here, look at my ID," she said, flashing her driver's license. "I drove all the way here from New York, by myself. Do you know how difficult that was? And now I get here and you say I can't see her because I'm not on any stupid lists? Please, can't you at least let her know I'm here? Surely, she'll approve my visit."

"Even if I let her know, she can't have any visits for another fifteen days. It's a policy for new transfers. She was just transferred down from Maximum, so I can tell you, no exceptions will be happening today. I can give you the address and you can try writing her, and I'm sure she'll add you on, since you're her sister and all. Ironically, she has another sister and brother-in-law listed, but not you. Wonder why? Seems a little 'unsisterly' if you ask me." The guard chuckled to her own amusement. "But right now, I'm gonna need for you to step out of the way because you're holding up the line."

Butterscotch looked behind her at the growing line, unsure what to do or say. "Well, can I have the information to write to her?" she asked, rolling her eyes as quickly as the guard turned to reach for a paper containing the address.

The guard wrote some numbers on the paper. "This is the inmate number you have to include when writing. You can check back in another fifteen days to see if you're on the list."

"So I have to sit in Kansas for fifteen days? I don't have any family or a place to stay here. Where am I supposed to go until then?"

"Ma'am, I'm not your social worker. I am not here to figure out all of your problems for you. If you're not willing to return to your home and then come back at that time, then go check into a hotel or something. They have cheap rooms for rent around town if you look. If you head into the bigger towns, expect to pay more than you would in the smaller towns. But next time, perhaps you'd do a bit of research before riding off halfcocked on two-day road trips, assuming it took you two days to journey down here, by yourself."

Butterscotch was beyond frustrated as she turned to leave. She had no idea where she would go or how she'd survive on the remaining $120 she had left until she received her next annuity payment from the lottery winnings that she benefited from, several years prior, when Chocolate played the winning numbers, and her sister, Tapioca, was placed in charge of the distribution of funds. In actuality, Butterscotch had made the long, desperate journey from New York to Kansas to see Chocolate, in hopes that Chocolate would release some of her portion of funds. In all the years that Chocolate was incarcerated in a maximum security prison for murdering their mother's killer, Butterscotch had only made three trips to see her sister, and each of those times, was when she had a need for money that no one else would help her with. Typically, Chocolate would instruct Tapioca to give Butterscotch something to hold her over. However, with Tapioca's recent suicide, and their youngest sister, Vanilla, quickly running off to marry Tapioca's widow, Butterscotch was left in a financial bind. Somehow, Vanilla and her new husband seemed to be in control of all the funds, and Butterscotch was unable to convince either to give her anything.

Year after year, Butterscotch had been living the glitz and glamourous life in New York City, and each year, she'd run out of funds before it was time for the next annuity. She'd always have to liquidate items to hold her over. Being placed in the same predicament year after year had failed to teach her any financial responsibility, until this last predicament… along with her approaching thirty in another year. At one point, she was filled with resentment about Tapioca not giving her the full share of the $130,000,000 jackpot that was won, especially after she took the cash payout. Tapioca set up one quarter each, of the payment in the form of annuity payments for both Vanilla and Butterscotch, and placed Chocolate's quarter in yet another account that only Tapioca had control of while Chocolate remained imprisoned. With several years of wasted dollars, and age starting to set in, Butterscotch was finally getting to a wiser place, and seeing the need to be more practical in her spending, so she wouldn't be broke and homeless, as her current dilemma finds her. She even asked to move to Utah to stay with Vanilla and her husband, Charles Webb. Charles was receptive to helping Butterscotch, but Vanilla was adamantly against providing any assistance to her irresponsible sister, hoping to teach her a lesson. So, her only hope in obtaining money, was by going to see Chocolate, and convincing her to make Vanilla give her some money.

Now being told she'd have to wait at least fifteen days just to visit, Butterscotch wasn't sure how she'd manage on the $120 and a gas card she had left to her name. Even worse, would be if Chocolate were to deny her any funds.

She drove about forty-five minutes from the prison, and found a country inn. She was hoping she could find a small town with someone generous enough to put her up for a few days. She went into the store and it seemed as if everyone got quiet as they turned to look at her, appearing out of place.

"Hello," she said with a plastered smile, feeling a bit intimidated, "I was wondering if someone could point me in the direction of anyone that's renting out a room for a few days or maybe a couple of weeks."

After some visual back and forth amongst the group of people, an elderly lady finally spoke up. "I believe there is a gentleman, about five or so miles from here, that might have some rooms. He has a big house and a barn."

At first the others seemed shocked by her speaking up to Butterscotch, but then they all seemed to have a changed expression of contentment on their faces, as they agreed.

The clerk spoke up, "Oh yeah, Ol' Mr. Hawkins. Fred Hawkins. He has plenty of space and plenty of land. His wife died about a year ago, so I'm sure he could use some help in exchange for a room. If you'd like, I can give him a call to let him know you're coming out."

"Oh my goodness. That would be so wonderful. Thank you. I could definitely help out however I can,"

Butterscotch said, totally excited.

Although the people seemed pleasant and helpful, she couldn't help but notice a few snickering, which caused her to feel a bit uncomfortable. She hoped it wasn't some type of trick, but then dismissed the notion when she thought about how it was an elderly woman who provided the information. It made no sense that the woman would be insincere, along with the store clerk.

The store clerk hung up the phone, and wrote on a piece of paper. "Here, this is the address. Mr. Fred is expecting you."

"Thank you so much. Thank you all."

"Let me warn you though, Fred can be kind of eccentric at times. You just have to not take anything personal. Sometimes he's really quiet and he'll just stare at you. He means no harm. He's a fifty-year-old harmless soul. He inherited all that land from his parents, and he never had any kids before his wife passed."

That made Butterscotch nervous. "You wouldn't happen to know of any women who might have a room available, would you?"

Everyone shook their heads as they hardly gave the question any thought.

"Can't think of anyone else in this town," the clerk answered. "This is a really small town and most homes here are filled with multiple generations under one roof. There's another town about ninety minutes away from here. Maybe you'll have better luck there."

Butterscotch tried to hide her disappointment, and smiled as she returned to her car. She looked at her gas tank and saw it was only half filled. She considered the drive to the next town, but then thought about how she had to spend very sparingly, which included gas as well. She decided to drive the five miles to Mr. Hawkins' home.

2

The land was huge, at least ten acres, and it was well kept. Somehow Butterscotch was expecting an unkempt land. Trees were few, but she was pleasantly surprised. As she drove up the long driveway leading to the house, she could see a man wearing overalls, sitting on the porch, rocking back and forth in a chair with his arms folded. His hair was completely white, and he looked as if he hadn't shaved in years. In actuality, the plump man appeared to be well over sixty-years-old. She was pretty certain the clerk said the man was fifty.

She got out of the car with a fake smile as she approached the front porch. "Hi Mr. Fred, I'm the young lady the clerk called you about for the room rental."

He stopped rocking and leaned forward in his seat. He straightened up his glasses on his face as he stared long and hard at Butterscotch.

"Are you a nigra?"

"Huh? A what?"

"A nigra. A black? You got blonde hair, but you look like a high yella nigra."

Butterscotch's jaw tightened. She's been called

many things in her life before, but never any derivative of the word, 'nigger.'

"You one of them Cajun girls?"

"My mother was white," Butterscotch partially lied. In fact, her mother was predominantly white, but since her mother was a former prostitute, there was no telling who her father was. It took Tapioca's death for her to learn that Charles was in fact Tapioca's father, and they were married with two children. Butterscotch was pretty certain that her father was also a black man, because her complexion was a hint yellower than Tapioca's. But because of their mother's mixed heritage, there was no telling. Somehow, Butterscotch had long flowing blonde hair, golden eyes, a high yellow complexion, an ample behind, with boastful breasts to match.

"What about your daddy?" Fred asked.

"I really never knew who my father was. I do know that my grandparents forbade my mother to date black men," she completely lied.

"Oh, okay," he said seeming content with the lie, as he resumed his rocking.

"I didn't ask how much you would charge me, but I really do not have any money. I only have $120 to last me until I find a job and get paid. However, I am willing to do whatever work you might need, to help offset some of the rent. I'm a hard worker, and I don't mind helping out or running errands."

"So you're saying you only have about $40 per week? It'll take you a few days to find a job, and about another two weeks to get your first pay."

"Well, I'm hoping to get some more money in a

couple of weeks. I could give you something extra then."

"The rent is $100 per week."

Butterscotch wanted to cry. She was beyond frustrated by her stressful day. The setting sun caused her even more frustration. "Could I give you $60 per week and then maybe work off the other $40? If I'm unable to pay you more by that time, I'll just be on my way."

"How you plan on working off your debt and trying to find a job?" he asked, staring at her as if he didn't believe her.

"Mr. Fred, I promise, I will do whatever it takes. I have nowhere to go tonight and I just drove here all the way from New York. I came to Kansas to see my sister, but I was unable to meet up with her. She won't be available until two weeks from now. I just really need to get through the two weeks."

For the first time, his eyes shifted to her thighs, causing her to shift her body in an effort to detract her assets.

"Anything?" he asked, as he leaned forward in his rocker again.

Butterscotch hoped he wasn't suggesting what she was thinking. At the same time, she thought about her alternatives. It wasn't like it would be the first time she had to do something unscrupulous to have a place to stay. It was almost becoming like a pattern, with each time she found herself broke and/or homeless, while she begged her sisters for additional funds.

"Sure, I can cook and clean. I've never worked on a

farm before, but I can help with that as well." She knew that wasn't the answer he was looking for, but was hoping that would suffice. She would be exceptionally angry to have to pay him rent and then give away her goodies to the old-looking, fifty-year-old.

"You can stay for $40 per week, but you'll have to pay the two weeks up front. We'll see how things go from there," he said, resuming his rocking again.

"Oh thank you! Thank you! I'll be sure to stay out of your way."

"That's good, because I don't like people in my way. I'm sure you'll have enough to keep you busy, anyhow."

Butterscotch smiled, "Sure thing. Should I go grab my bag from the car now and take it to my room?"

Fred got up from his rocker and stepped off of the porch to go to the car to grab her bag. She was impressed with his manners.

As he got closer, he looked at her bottom in more detail. "You sure you ain't a nigra? You look kind of full down there."

She hated being referred to as a 'nigra' but she couldn't afford to get caught up in her feelings, as her alternative would be sleeping in her car again, and she was in great need of a good hot shower.

"I had the surgery. I wanted to have more," she lied.

"Your skin is very yella."

"I went to a tanning salon about a month ago and my skin has never been right since then," she lied again.

He smiled and nodded. "Just goes to show you ain't supposed to be trying to look like them."

"I have definitely been regretting it."

"You a natural blonde?"

"Yes, sir. No hair colors. My mother's hair was actually a pinkish blonde."

"That's great. Now let's get you inside so you can get situated."

He grabbed her bag from the trunk and escorted her to her room in the large, immaculate home. Her smile faded as he dropped her bag in a nicely furnished room that had no door directly across from what appeared to be his room. She was pretty certain that there had to be another room she could have had, one with a door.

"Uh, Mr. Fred, would you happen to have a room with a door available?"

"NO!" he sharply replied. "If you don't want this, you can be on your way."

Butterscotch was screaming inside, but then tried to convince herself that this would be no different than one of the shelters she's had to stay in, a time or two, when she'd run out of money.

"Okay, this is fine. It's a beautiful room," she said trying to get back into his good grace.

"That'll be $80 to cover this week and next," he said, holding out his hand.

Well damn! she thought to herself. He wasn't giving her any minute to get comfortable, but then she couldn't blame him, because she was a stranger.

She dug into her purse and pulled together the $80. He looked over her shoulder, as if he wanted to see how much she really had. She turned to give him the money, and she ran right into him, dropping the bills from her hand. She bent to pick it up and put it in his hand. After he left her room, she looked around and noticed no fan or air conditioner. She was apprehensive about asking, but since it was at least ninety-degrees outside, she couldn't imagine how she'd survive a night in that heat.

"Mr. Fred, would you happen to have an extra fan I could use tonight? The room is rather warm," she asked, catching up with him before he made it back down the stairs.

"I don't have an extra fan. You'll have to open up the window. There'll be good air coming through it."

She was very disappointed, but tried to mask it with a smile.

"I'll have dinner fixed shortly. You might wanna go get yourself cleaned up. Starting tomorrow, you can cook the meals."

"That'll be great. Could you point me in the direction of the bathroom so I could get a shower?"

"I have a shower, but I'd prefer you use the tub to keep from wasting water. And don't fill that tub up high," he answered as he led her to the upstairs bathroom.

As luck would have it, although there was a door to the bathroom, there was no lock.

She succeeded in getting her bath without any interruptions. She began to think maybe he wasn't as bad as she thought. She did feel uncomfortable when she realized the only garments she packed were short shorts, miniskirts, tank tops and one extra pair of jeans, beside the ones she had worn that day. There were only two bras and all thongs, packed with her nightgown. She didn't want to appear to entice Mr. Fred. Generally, she didn't sleep in nightgowns or underwear, but only brought the one gown just in case she needed to sleep somewhere that wasn't private.

Dinner consisted of beans, spinach and possum. She had never had possum before in her life, and she wasn't planning to start on that day, despite it smelling delicious.

"I have never had possum before. I don't know if it would be a good idea to put much on my plate. I would hate to waste it."

"Around here, we don't waste. I'm sure you'll enjoy it or learn to enjoy it," he stated, as if she had no choice but to eat whatever he gave her.

She accepted her plate with a smile. She was surprised when he took her hands to say grace before allowing them to eat. Several times as she ate of the possum, she felt as if she would regurgitate. She didn't want to anger him, so she fought to keep it down. After dinner, he served her a slice of warmed, store-bought, apple pie and vanilla ice cream. Butterscotch hated vanilla ice cream for the mere fact that she couldn't stand her sister, Vanilla, with the same name. Again, she had to fight to keep from throwing it up. When Fred was done, he got up from the table and left the kitchen, without saying a word, leaving all the dishes and pots. Butterscotch didn't know if he was coming back or if she should just go on and take the initiative to clean the kitchen. She did the latter, and he hadn't returned. He was in the living room watching his fifty-inch, flat screened television mounted over his stone fireplace.

He sat in an oversized rocker-recliner, and gently rocked. When Butterscotch was done with the kitchen, she didn't know if she should join him in the living room to make small talk or steer clear, since she promised to stay out of his way.

"The kitchen is all cleaned up, and everything is put away. Is there a particular time you like to have your breakfast in the mornings?" she asked from the doorway.

She felt his eyes fixated on her hips and thighs again, causing her to feel grossly underdressed in the shorts and tee shirt.

"I usually go get fresh eggs and milk from the barn around six, and then fix my breakfast, but you can fix it when I return."

"Cool. And do you drink coffee with your breakfast?" she asked, still fidgeting with her shorts, to try making them longer.

"Sure do."

"Great! I'll go on and retire for the evening so I can get up early to fix breakfast," she said with an uneasy smile.

"But I'm about to prepare my bath."

"Huh?"

"I'm about to prepare my bath," he repeated. "I need you to scrub my back."

"Huh?" she gulped. "Your back? But how?"

"I have a back scrubber, but it's kind of hard to use it. I have a hard time reaching around with it. I mean, if it's a problem, just say so," he said as suggesting that she better not have a problem with scrubbing his back.

"It's not a problem," she answered in defeat.

He smiled, got up from his chair after turning off his television, and then headed up the stairs to run his bath.

Butterscotch was thankful that she wasn't summoned to the bathroom until after his six-foot-three, plump frame was already squeezed into the tub. He handed her his scrub brush when she entered.

"I probably got some blackheads back there that I need you to take out. Look up in the medicine cabinet and get the tweezers and some witch hazel."

Again, Butterscotch was feeling the urge to vomit. In her mind, the blackhead removals were worth at least a month of rent, but she survived it, along with scrubbing his back. She hurried from the bathroom before he would stand up, exposing his privates.

She returned to her room, debating on whether or not to change into her nightgown. The room was so hot, she had no idea how she'd be able to sleep. Every once in a while, a nice little breeze would blow through the window. She decided to quickly change into her nightgown, since she felt she'd be most comfortable in it, with the heat. As she climbed into her bed, she realized she had a direct birds-eye view of his bed. She was hoping she wouldn't have to witness him doing anything to himself.

He walked into his room wearing his pajamas and a robe. She watched from her dark room as he removed his robe and climbed into his bed, turning on his television. After he turned off his room light, she laid wondering how she'd ever be able to fall asleep in that heat.

She deliriously opened her eyes, unaware of ever dozing off. She saw Fred standing in the dark, just watching her. The image startled her, causing her to jump up, but then realizing Fred was actually in his own room. Even more startling, she witnessed Fred pleasuring himself underneath his cover. She quickly turned away, not wanting to watch. She laid on her side, watching the stars outside of the window until she eventually dozed off again. That time she was awakened to a sensual sensation, while lying on her stomach. She felt a hand rubbing between her thighs. More specifically, the hand seemed to be in pursuit of her wetness. She laid still as she attempted to process the reality of what was happening, or if it was yet more delirium as a result of the heat. Her mind eventually registered the act as real.

His fingers were gentle. Although she hated the idea of what he was doing to her, she knew in the back of her mind to expect some perversion on his part. If anything, she was trying not to enjoy the sensation that was making her vaginal walls throb. It had been over two weeks since she was last touched by a man, and that was when she was able to get a thousand dollars to help her survive until she was able to get to see Chocolate and get more funds. Although she'd had sex for money on many occasions, she would never refer to herself as being a prostitute like her mother. However, she did feel that since her mother blessed her with the physical assets, she would make them work for her when necessary.

He gently rolled Butterscotch from her stomach onto

her back and spread her thighs apart. She played as if she were still asleep and unaware. He continued to rub her wet spot, further stimulating her clitoris. The good sensation was making it more difficult to play possum. With his free hand, he slightly moved her gown from over her one of her breasts, and took a nipple to gently suck. It was getting even harder to contain the sensation, but she didn't want to give him the impression that she was an awakened, willing participant. Then he would climb on top of her, so she continued to fight the urge. Instead, she tried to think of angry thoughts, to help resist her wanting to raise her hips to cause his fingers to go deep inside of her.

He abruptly stopped and returned to his room. She laid still, wondering if he was going to return. She thought maybe he was going to get a condom or something. A cool breeze hit her exposed, wet nipple, making her even hornier. She waited and waited, but he never returned. The next three nights were a repeat of the same, with her having to wash his back, him going to his room to pleasure himself, and him sneaking in during the night to get his feels on her. However, the following night, things took a turn.

Butterscotch Pudding Next Door: (Available in late 2019)

© 2017 – The Queen

www.ingramcontent.com/pod-product-compliance
Lightning Source LLC
Chambersburg PA
CBHW032023120726

47898CB00002BB/626